WHO IS NO-NAME'S REAL OWNER?

A roar went up from the rest of the crowd, and Lisa quickly turned her attention back to the race, forgetting all about the girl who seemed so interested in Stevie and her horse. Joey Dutton was crossing the finish line yards ahead of his closest competitor. Lisa cheered, her voice almost lost among the others around her.

But a moment later one voice could be heard above the rest, shrill and angry.

"That's my horse!" the blond girl cried, pushing her way to the front of the crowd and pointing at No-Name. "That's my horse!"

THE SADDLE CLUB

GIFT HORSE

BONNIE BRYANT

A SKYLARK BOOK
NEW YORK · TORONTO · LONDON · SYDNEY · AUCKLAND

Many thanks to Lisa Scott of Breyer
Horses for her help and expertise.

RL 5, 009–012

GIFT HORSE
A Bantam Skylark Book / January 1995

Skylark Books is a registered trademark of Bantam Books,
a division of Bantam Doubleday Dell Publishing Group, Inc.
Registered in U.S. Patent and Trademark Office and elsewhere.

"The Saddle Club" is a trademark of Bonnie Bryant Hiller.
The Saddle Club design/logo, which consists of an inverted
U-shaped design, a riding crop, and a riding hat, is a
trademark of Bantam Books.

ISBN 0-553-48156-8

Published simultaneously in the United States and Canada

Bantam Books are published by Bantam Books, a division of Bantam
Doubleday Dell Publishing Group, Inc. Its trademark, consisting of the
words "Bantam Books" and the portrayal of a rooster, is Registered in U.S.
Patent and Trademark Office and in other countries. Marca Registrada.
Bantam Books, 1540 Broadway, New York, New York 10036.

PRINTED IN THE UNITED STATES OF AMERICA

OPM   0 9 8 7 6 5 4 3 2

*I would like to express my special thanks
to Catherine Hapka for her help
in the writing of this book.*

1

"THE EYE PATCH, Veronica! Don't forget the eye patch!" called Stevie Lake frantically.

"Oops!" Veronica diAngelo took her foot out of the stirrup and headed back to the cardboard box on the ground. Veronica was one of the most stylish and fashion-conscious girls Stevie knew—but at this precise moment nobody would ever have guessed it. She had hurriedly pulled on loose red pants and a black vest over her riding clothes, and a black felt pirate's hat was jammed over her hard hat.

Stevie held her breath and glanced over at the other Pony Club teams competing in the costume relay race. This was the last leg of the race, and the top three teams' scores were so close that the order of finish would decide which team won the day's competition. She saw that two of the seven other racers were already mounted and riding toward the finish line. The crowd was cheering wildly. If Veronica didn't hurry, Stevie's team wouldn't stand a chance of winning.

Veronica grabbed the black eye patch from the bottom of the costume box and snapped it on over her head. "Sorry about that, guys," she called to her teammates as she mounted her Arabian mare, Garnet, and took off.

Stevie shot a surprised look at her other two teammates, who also happened to be her two best friends, Carole Hanson and Lisa Atwood. They returned the look. If there was one thing Veronica diAngelo was *not* known for, it was being a team player. If there was one thing she *was* known for, it was never apologizing for anything she did—or taking responsibility for it, for that matter. In fact, Veronica had been suspended several times from Horse Wise, the chapter of the U.S. Pony Club based at Pine Hollow Stable, where the girls all rode. Because the diAngelos were the wealthiest family in their hometown of Willow Creek, Virginia, Veronica thought she didn't have to follow the same rules other people did. That attitude had gotten her in trouble more than once with Max Regnery, the owner of Pine Hollow and director of Horse Wise. As far as he was concerned, rules were made to be obeyed—even if you were Veronica diAngelo.

Carole, Stevie, and Lisa couldn't imagine ever being suspended from Horse Wise. Riding was very important to all of them. In fact, it was so important that they had formed The Saddle Club, which had only two rules: Members had to be horse crazy, and they had to be willing to help one another out in any way necessary. In addition to the three girls, there were several out-of-town members, including Stevie's boyfriend, Phil Marsten, who lived in a nearby town and was a member of Cross County, one of the Pony Club teams competing today. According to Stevie, Carole, and Lisa, The Saddle Club was a perfect organization, since it was the perfect combination of horses and friendship.

They all thought the U.S. Pony Club was a pretty great organization, too. One of the things the Pony Club did was sponsor rallies like the one that day. But the most important goal of the organization was to teach young members about every aspect of horse care. That meant riding, of course, but it also meant stable management, veterinary care, and all kinds of other things. Although some of the things they learned were definitely more interesting than others, The Saddle Club thought that learning everything they could about horses made riding even more fun.

They wouldn't have expected Veronica to agree with them, though. She was never very enthusiastic about Horse Wise, even when she wasn't on suspension. Stevie, Carole, and Lisa had been dismayed when Max had assigned Veronica to their team for the two local rallies being held this weekend and the next. But much to their surprise, Veronica had been more bearable than usual. For some reason

3

she didn't seem interested in her two favorite activities—complaining and bragging. Instead, she actually seemed as eager to do well at the rally as her teammates were. Despite her faults, Veronica was a better-than-average rider. When she paid attention and did her best, she added a lot to the team.

"She's catching up," Carole cried excitedly, jostling Stevie with her elbow.

"Go, Garnet, go," Lisa chanted.

Stevie just held her breath and watched as eight horses cantered toward the finish line at the other end of the ring. Seconds later the race was over. Veronica and Garnet had done their best to make up ground, but they ended placing third in the race—which meant the Horse Wise team finished third overall. A team called Fairfax came in first, and Cross County was second.

"Oh well," Lisa said philosophically as the girls waited for Veronica to rejoin them. "Third out of eight teams isn't bad at all."

"And we weren't bad at all, either," Carole added. "In fact, we were pretty great."

"But Cross County was a little greater, weren't they?" Stevie said, frowning just a little as she patted her horse, a spirited, part-Arabian bay mare her parents had recently bought for her. Stevie hadn't decided on the perfect name for her new horse yet, so for the time being she was calling her No-Name. No-Name tossed her head and snorted, staring across the ring at the finish line. "See? No-Name agrees," Stevie said. "She thinks we should have won."

Carole and Lisa exchanged glances. They could guess what was on Stevie's mind. Stevie and her boyfriend, Phil, had a lot in common—including a competitive streak a mile wide. Once Stevie got it in her head that Phil thought he might be better than her in some way—especially if that way involved riding—she wouldn't rest until she'd proven him wrong. Her competitiveness had come between them more than once. It had come between Stevie and her friends a few times, too.

Lisa decided it was time to change the subject and take Stevie's mind off Phil. "No-Name sure was wonderful today, Stevie," she said. "Especially considering it was the first time you two were competing together."

"She was great, wasn't she?" Stevie agreed, suddenly all smiles again. She gave the mare a hug. No-Name snorted and nibbled on Stevie's long dark-blond ponytail. Even though she'd owned No-Name for only a few weeks, Stevie couldn't imagine how either of them had ever gotten along without each other. They had similar personalities, mischievous and independent. It made No-Name a challenge to ride at times, but it also meant that Stevie could usually figure out the best way to handle her. "It feels as though I've been riding her for ages. And she's good at these games. She really seems to like them."

Just then Veronica trotted up on Garnet. She dismounted and pulled off the pirate hat and eye patch. "Hey, don't you think you guys are a little overdressed for this occasion?" she remarked as she stepped out of the loose red costume pants and tossed them into the box.

Stevie, Carole, and Lisa glanced at one another and burst out laughing. In the excitement of Veronica's finish, none of them had bothered to remove the costumes they'd put on for their legs of the race. Carole was wearing a red clown nose and a baggy spotted jumpsuit. Stevie was outfitted as a baby, complete with a bib and a frilly white bonnet. And Lisa wore the hat, bandanna, and chaps of a cowgirl.

"Thanks for the fashion tip, Veronica," Stevie said, pulling off the bib. As the words left her mouth, she thought they sounded familiar, and she thought she knew why. She had said the same thing to the spoiled rich girl plenty of other times when Veronica had made fun of Stevie's faded jeans or dusty riding boots. But this time Stevie wasn't being sarcastic—at least not in the same way. Because this time she knew that Veronica was laughing *with* her rather than *at* her.

Once all four girls' costumes were back in the box, they led their horses toward their temporary stalls in Linton Stables' big barn. Different local Pony Clubs took turns hosting the rallies. Today's it was at Linton. Cross County was hosting a larger rally the following Saturday.

No-Name pranced along the whole way to her stall, her intelligent eyes taking in everything around her.

As soon as all the horses were comfortable, Stevie, Carole, Lisa, and Veronica rejoined the rest of the Horse Wise team. It included several other members of the girls' intermediate riding class, as well as a team of younger riders known as the Pony Tails. Right now, all the riders were milling around the grassy area behind the barn where Pine Hollow's horse vans and cars were parked. Max was standing near the open back door of his station wagon with his mother, universally known as Mrs. Reg. The two of them were doing their best to hand out the sandwiches and sodas they'd brought, but they were having a hard time keeping up with the demands from the hungry riders.

Once Stevie, Carole, and Lisa had received their food, they found a shady spot away from the others and sat down to eat.

"We've got to think of ways to improve before next week's rally," said Stevie. She was still thinking about their third-place finish—or more accurately, their second-to-Phil finish.

Lisa swallowed a bite of peanut-butter sandwich. "We didn't really make any bad mistakes," she pointed out. "I mean, I did drop my egg once in the egg-and-spoon race, and Veronica forgot her eye patch, but those weren't major errors."

"True," Carole agreed. "Cross County was just a little sharper, that's all."

Stevie nodded. "That's why *we* have to get sharper before next weekend," she said firmly. "We'll have to put in some extra practice time. I hope Veronica's agreeable mood continues for a while."

"Me, too," Carole said. "And not just because of the rally. She's really a lot more pleasant to be around when she's not being snotty and superior every second. I haven't seen her act this nice since Thanksgiving." Veronica had spent the holiday with Carole and her father the year before when Veronica's parents had had to leave the country on business. Carole had been surprised to discover that the spoiled little rich girl actually had a human side. Unfortunately, as soon as the visit had ended, so had Veronica's friendly mood.

"Definitely," Stevie said. "I wonder what's up with her these days." She took a long swig of soda.

"I think I may have an idea about that," Lisa commented. "I overheard my father telling my mother that Mr. diAngelo's bank is in some kind of serious trouble."

"What does that mean?" Carole asked.

Lisa shrugged. "From the way my dad was talking, it sounded as though it might have to shut down."

"Wow. That would mean Mr. diAngelo would lose his job," Carole said slowly.

"And all his money," Stevie added, with just a hint of a

smirk. "Can you imagine that? Poor Veronica would have to give up her weekly trips to the mall. . . ."

"And her chauffeured Mercedes," Lisa put in.

"And her designer riding clothes," Carole finished. "Then she'll have to start dressing like you, Stevie."

Stevie and Lisa laughed. Even if Veronica had been acting nicer lately, they couldn't work up much sympathy for her predicament.

"Hey, is there room for one more at this table?" Phil Marsten asked, walking up to them.

"Sure," Stevie said with a smile. "Pull up a chair."

"Thanks." Phil dropped to the grass beside Stevie and began unwrapping his sandwich. "You all did great today," he told the three girls.

"Not as great as you did," Lisa replied honestly. "But thanks."

Carole nodded in agreement. But out of the corner of her eye she could see Stevie's face, and she didn't like what she saw. There was a definite competitive glint in Stevie's eye.

Luckily Phil changed the subject to ask about No-Name, who had been a temporary boarder in his family's barn before moving to Pine Hollow. Soon he and Stevie were chatting easily together about how much the mare had seemed to enjoy the day's events.

But Carole couldn't help remembering some of the times Stevie's competitive nature had gotten her in trouble in the past. Once Max had decided to teach them to play polocrosse, a combination of polo and lacrosse. Stevie had ended up practicing so hard for a game against Phil's team that she'd injured her ankle. Still wanting to be a part of the competition, she'd volunteered to coach the team. But she had been so demanding that the whole team was ready to quit before long.

That experience had turned out just fine in the end, Carole reminded herself. Once Stevie had figured out how impossible she was being, she had turned into an excellent coach. Maybe by next weekend, Stevie would realize coming in first wasn't important and forget all about coming in third today.

After lunch it was time for the younger riders to compete. Stevie had volunteered to coach the team made up of Pine Hollow's youngest riders. She knew she'd done a good job, too. The team was enthusiastic and well prepared for every race. Stevie watched from her position on No-Name's back, shouting encouragement and advice the whole time. Under Stevie's expert guidance, the team came in first or second in almost every event, from the water-balloon toss to the blindfolded relay race.

Carole and Lisa cheered from the sidelines as the competitors lined up for their last event, the classic egg-and-spoon relay. All around them the other spectators were just as enthusiastic. It was fun watching the young riders, because they were so obviously having fun themselves. But no one seemed to be having more fun than Stevie and No-Name.

"Go, May!" Stevie shouted from the sidelines as the race started. She bounced up and down excitedly in No-Name's saddle. "You can do it!"

May Grover didn't look around at Stevie—that would have broken her concentration—but Lisa saw the young girl nod with determination. Lisa smiled. Stevie really was a good coach. It was obvious that the team wanted to do well for her as well as for themselves. Lisa started cheering even louder as May reached the end of the ring and carefully handed her spoon to the next rider, Jasmine James. The pass-off went effortlessly, and Jasmine rode her pony back across the ring at a smooth walk, well ahead of the other teams.

Just then Lisa noticed one person in the crowd who wasn't cheering. A girl was standing silently nearby, staring intently at something in the ring. She was a little older than Lisa, with short blond hair, and she was wearing riding clothes. Lisa recognized her as a member of the Mendenhall Stables' Pony Club, but she didn't know her name. When Lisa followed her gaze, she realized the older girl was staring at Stevie and No-Name with a decidedly odd look on her face.

A roar went up from the rest of the crowd, and Lisa quickly turned her attention back to the race, forgetting all about the girl who seemed so interested in Stevie and her horse. Joey Dutton was crossing the finish line yards ahead of his closest competitor. Lisa cheered, her voice almost lost among the others around her.

But a moment later one voice could be heard above the rest, shrill and angry.

"That's my horse!" the blond girl cried, pushing her way to the front of the crowd and pointing at No-Name. "That's my horse!"

2

Out on the field, Stevie was vaguely aware of the blond girl in the crowd, who was pointing at her and shouting something about No-Name. It almost sounded as though she was yelling that No-Name was her horse. But Stevie didn't pay much attention—she was too busy congratulating her victorious team.

Besides, there was no doubt that No-Name was Stevie's horse. The Lakes had bought the mare from Mr. Baker, the director of the Cross County Pony Club, a few weeks earlier. And Stevie knew beyond a shadow of a doubt that the spirited mare was meant to be hers forever.

Stevie was crazy about a lot of horses. One of her favorites was a skewbald pony named Stewball who lived on her friend Kate's dude ranch out west. Stevie also loved Car-

ole's horse Starlight; Topside, Max's Thoroughbred gelding; and just about every other horse she'd ever met.

But now Stevie knew that none of those horses could
ever belong to her the way No-Name did. The two of them
were perfectly matched in personality. Where another rider
might get annoyed at the mare's curiosity and playfulness,
Stevie loved it. Where another horse might get confused at
Stevie's impulsive commands during mounted games, No-
Name seemed to know what Stevie was thinking almost
before Stevie did. Like Stevie, No-Name also had a talent
for dressage, a form of riding requiring precision, skill, and
careful training. Not every horse had that kind of talent—
and not every rider, either.

"That's my horse!" the shout came again. Stevie glanced
at the girl, who had short blond hair and an angry look on
her face. Then she returned her attention to her team,
helping the excited girls and boy lead their ponies out of
the ring.

Carole and Lisa were there a moment later to greet and
help her.

"What was that girl shouting about?" Stevie asked them
as they headed into the barn.

Carole and Lisa both shrugged.

"Something about you and No-Name," Carole replied.

Before any of them could say another word, May Grover
rushed up to Stevie with her pony trailing behind her.
"Stevie, will you help me find a hoof pick? I lost mine."

"Sure thing," Stevie replied instantly. With that, the three older girls forgot all about the blond girl and set to work assisting the younger girls with their horses. There was a lot to do to get the horses ready for the trip back to Pine Hollow, which meant there was no time to waste thinking about strange girls yelling odd things in the crowd.

A few minutes later Carole was leading Diablo out of the barn toward the van when she passed Red O'Malley, Pine Hollow's head stable hand. His normally cheerful face wore a puzzled expression.

"What's the matter, Red?" Carole asked, immediately concerned. Ever since she'd owned Starlight, she knew better than ever how easy it was for things to go wrong with a horse. Spotting problems or potential problems quickly was one of the skills Max tried to teach them in Horse Wise. Carole was good at it. So was Stevie. For instance, Stevie had been the one to figure out No-Name's allergy to weeds, thereby saving the mare a lot of unnecessary discomfort.

Red shook his head. "Nothing's the matter," he replied, reaching out to take Diablo's lead. "At least, I don't think so. But you'd better go take a look for yourself." He gestured toward the row of temporary stalls behind him.

Carole hurried in the direction he'd indicated, still feeling a little worried. A voice came out to greet her—Veronica's voice.

"That's right, Jessica," Veronica was saying from inside

15

one of the stalls. "If you need to walk around behind him, you should run your hand over his back and quarters, move slowly, and talk to him the whole time. That way he knows what you're doing, and he's less likely to get spooked. See?"

Carole smiled, understanding why Red had looked so shocked. One of Pine Hollow's many traditions was that riders helped care for the horses they rode. That meant grooming, cleaning tack, mucking out stalls, and everything else that had to be done. Another tradition was that riders helped each other whenever necessary. Both traditions were ones that Veronica liked to ignore. Normally she seemed to consider Red her own personal stable hand, and the last place anyone would expect to find her was helping someone else.

But now, here she was helping out another rider. Carole shook her head. Had Veronica really turned over a new leaf this time? Then another thought occurred to her, and her smile faded a little. Did this change of heart have anything to do with the rumors about her father's bank?

Before she could think about that any further, she heard footsteps behind her. She turned to see Stevie and Lisa approaching. Lisa was leading Prancer, the lovely Thoroughbred mare she usually rode, and Stevie was carrying Prancer's grooming bucket. The grooming bucket contained all the grooming tools Lisa would need, including brushes and combs, sponges, rags, a hoof pick and oil, and an extra lead line. Each horse at Pine Hollow had a grooming bucket, and the riders were supposed to make sure the buckets remained clean and fully stocked. Having everything in one place was especially helpful during trips like this, but it also made things easier back at Pine Hollow.

"What's the big idea?" Stevie demanded with mock seriousness. "How can you stand around here daydreaming while the rest of us are working?" She put her hands on her hips in imitation of one of Max's favorite poses.

Carole giggled. "If you think that's weird, just listen." She nodded toward the stall where Veronica, still oblivious to their presence, was giving Jessica tips on watching a horse's ears to figure out his mood.

Lisa's eyes widened. "This is almost spooky!" she whispered.

"I know," Carole agreed. "I was just wondering whether Mr. diAngelo's money troubles have anything to do with this new and improved Veronica."

Stevie shrugged. "Well, whatever the reason is, let's not mention anything to Veronica. After all, we don't want to make her self-conscious about how nice and helpful she's being these days. You know what they say about never looking a gift horse in the mouth. She might stop!"

The others laughed and agreed. Just then Stevie spotted Phil approaching and smiled. "Hi," she called to him happily. "You're just in time. We were just going to get No-Name and load her up for the trip back."

"We were?" Lisa said, but Stevie and Phil didn't hear

17

her. The two of them were already heading down the aisle toward No-Name's temporary stall, chatting enthusiastically. Lisa and Carole exchanged smiles and shrugged.

"I guess when she said 'we,' she meant herself and Phil," Carole said with a laugh. "Come on, I'll give you a hand with Prancer." The two of them headed in the opposite direction.

When Stevie and Phil arrived at No-Name's stall, Stevie opened the door and started to go inside. "Hi there, you big beautiful hor . . ."

Her voice trailed off, and she backed quickly out of the stall. "Hey, what are you doing in there?" she demanded, her voice hard and suspicious.

"What's wrong, Stevie?" Phil immediately stepped to her side and peered over the stall's half door. The blond girl from the crowd was standing in the stall, staring at No-Name. No-Name was staring back calmly. "Who are you?" Phil asked, puzzled.

Stevie crossed her arms over her chest and glared at the stranger. "What are you doing in there?" she snapped before the girl could answer Phil's question. "That's my horse, you know." Stevie didn't like the look on the other girl's face. She looked happy to see No-Name. No, more than happy—she looked *relieved*. Stevie couldn't imagine why, and she didn't really want to know.

"Where did you get this horse?" the blond girl demanded. She held out her hand and No-Name reached forward to nuzzle it, obviously hoping for a treat.

"If you must know, my parents bought her for me," Stevie replied curtly. "As I said, she's my horse, and I'll thank you to leave her alone. You'd better get out of her stall before she hurts you."

"She won't hurt me," the girl replied confidently. "She knows me. Because she's *my* horse." To Stevie's astonishment, the stranger stepped forward and gave No-Name a big hug. No-Name lowered her head to snuffle at the girl's hair, as if the mare were returning the hug as best she could.

Stevie watched, speechless, as the girl quietly let herself out of the stall, closing the door carefully behind her. She hurried away down the aisle without another word.

As soon as the stranger disappeared around a corner, Stevie opened the door and entered the stall. The vision of her horse nuzzling the strange girl was stamped on her mind. "Sorry about that, No-Name," Stevie murmured. She reached out to hug the horse, and felt No-Name's soft nose on her hair. It was obvious that the mare was happy to see her. But she'd seemed happy to see the other girl, too, and that bothered Stevie.

Maybe she just mistook that girl for me, Stevie thought. She nodded a little to herself, sure that that had to be the explanation.

"What's going on?" Phil asked. "Why does that girl think No-Name is her horse?"

"What's taking you guys so long?" Carole interrupted. "We're almost ready to go. Where's Stevie?"

"Something weird just happened," Phil replied.

Stevie stuck her head out over the half door. "I'm in here," she called to her friend. "And Phil's right. Something very weird just happened."

Carole picked up No-Name's grooming bucket and let herself into the stall with Stevie. "Well, tell me about it while we get her ready to go," she suggested. "Max is itching to get back."

"I'd better take off," Phil said. "My teammates might think I'm some kind of traitor if they catch me here helping the competition." He took a few steps, then paused and looked back. "Even if you guys weren't much competition for us today," he added teasingly. He hurried away.

Ordinarily that would have brought a strong and immediate reaction from Stevie. But today she didn't even seem to hear Phil's remark.

Carole watched her friend with concern.

"What's wrong?" she asked.

Stevie described the encounter with the strange girl. "And then she said No-Name was her horse, and she hugged her," Stevie finished. "And No-Name let her do it."

Carole picked up a brush to give No-Name a quick

20

once-over. "Is that all?" she said. "I'm sure that girl was mistaken. A lot of bays look alike."

Stevie raised her eyebrows. "Like this?" she said, pointing at No-Name. A white marking shaped like an upside-down exclamation point ran down the mare's face to her nose. Her two left legs were white to the knee, while the socks on her right legs extended only to her fetlocks.

Carole shrugged. "Why not?" she replied.

It wasn't much of an answer, but it made Stevie feel better. "I guess you're right," she said. "That girl must be imagining things."

Carole nodded. "Well, I don't want to try to imagine what Max will say to us if we don't get *this* girl loaded up pretty soon," she cautioned. Max was not famous for his patience.

But having decided to forget about the mysterious blond girl, Stevie had just remembered something else. "Can you believe that Phil?" she demanded as she opened the stall door and led No-Name out.

"What?" Carole asked, a little surprised as always by the speed with which Stevie's mind could switch topics. She grabbed No-Name's grooming bucket and joined Stevie by the mare's head. "What did Phil do?"

"Didn't you hear that crack he made about Horse Wise not being much competition?" Stevie reminded her. She shook her head angrily. "After all, the scores were pretty darn close. And didn't the younger team come in first place? I suppose that means nothing, hmm?"

Carole held back a smile. This sounded more like her friend. "I think he was just kidding, Stevie," she said, trying to sound tactful.

Stevie smiled grimly. "Well, we'll see who has the last laugh next weekend," she said. "With another whole week of practice, No-Name and I will be unbeatable."

The mare suddenly shook her head and snorted, as if in response to Stevie's comment. Carole shook her head, too. She had a feeling it was going to be an interesting week.

A BUSY HOUR and a half later, things were almost back to normal at Pine Hollow Stable. The Saddle Club had settled their horses in for the night and helped the younger riders to do the same.

Lisa poked her head into Starlight's stall, where Carole was feeding the gelding carrot slices. "Have you cleaned your saddle yet?" she asked. She was carrying Prancer's saddle.

"Not yet," Carole replied as Starlight carefully lifted the last of the carrots from her open hand with his soft lips. "I haven't had a spare moment until right now."

"I know what you mean," Lisa said. She held the door for Carole and then the girls headed for the tack room with their dirty saddles. As they passed No-Name's stall, which was right next to Starlight's, they looked in to see if Stevie was there. She wasn't. Lisa gave No-Name's nose a quick pat. During the ride back to Pine Hollow Stevie had filled Lisa in on what had happened with the girl from the other Pony Club. It was so strange to think someone actually believed No-Name belonged to her.

Stevie's friends found her a moment later when they entered the tack room. Stevie was already hard at work cleaning No-Name's saddle. She looked up as Carole and Lisa entered. "Hi there," she greeted them. "How about a Saddle Club meeting at TD's when we finish here?"

"Sound's good to me," Carole replied, and Lisa nodded. TD's, also known as Tastee Delight, was the ice cream parlor at the local shopping center. Although Saddle Club meetings could happen just about anyplace, TD's was one of the best places to have them.

As Lisa set down her saddle, she noticed that the saddle on the next rack hadn't been cleaned. "Hey, you guys, check this out," she commented. "Garnet's saddle sure could use a good workout with some saddle soap."

Stevie raised her eyebrows. "You're not suggesting *we* do something about it, are you?" she asked.

"No way," Lisa replied. "But this just proves that Veronica hasn't had a total personality transplant or anything. Even if she's improved enough to bring her own saddle to the tack room, she's still too much herself to actually *clean* it."

24

Carole laughed. "That's right," she said. "I hadn't really thought about it until now, but she *did* disappear about five seconds after the vans got back here—before any of the serious work started. It's almost a relief somehow."

"True," Stevie agreed, stopping her scrubbing and leaning back to give her arm a rest. "At least we know Veronica hasn't been taken over by aliens, like in that movie *Invasion of the Body Snatchers.*"

The others started laughing. At that moment, Mrs. Reg came out of her office, which opened onto the tack room. She eyed the giggling girls, then surveyed their tack. "You missed a spot, Lisa," she said at last, pointing to Lisa's saddle.

"Oops," said Lisa, her cheeks reddening a little. "Thanks, Mrs. Reg." The girls knew that Mrs. Reg didn't mind hearing them talking and joking when they worked—as long as they really were working. All three of them buckled down to prove that they were.

Mrs. Reg stood watching them for a few more seconds. Then she said, "I just had a rather curious phone call about you, Stevie."

"Really?" Stevie said, looking a little worried. "It wasn't my school, was it?" One of Max's strictest rules was that grades came before horses. Stevie sometimes came dangerously close to getting in trouble on that account.

"No, nothing like that," Mrs. Reg replied. "It was the father of one of the girls on the Mendenhall Pony Club

25

team. He was asking about the girl from Pine Hollow who has a bay mare, part Arabian, with uneven socks and an upside down exclamation point on her face."

"Hey, maybe he's some kind of talent scout or something," Lisa said excitedly. "Stevie, you and No-Name were really in top form today. Maybe he wants to sign you up and make you rich and famous."

But Carole was frowning. "I doubt it, Lisa," she said. "It's more likely it was the father of that girl who kept saying No-Name was her horse."

Lisa's face fell. "Oh, that's right," she said.

Stevie gulped, and the memory of the blond girl hugging No-Name popped back into her mind. "Why would her father be calling?" she asked. "After all, no matter what that girl claims, my parents paid good money for No-Name. She belongs to me, fair and square."

"It's probably nothing," Mrs. Reg said. "If the girl has lost her horse, she's probably so worried she can't see straight. A lot of horses look alike. She's just mistaken, that's all."

"I hope so," Stevie said, relieved at Mrs. Reg's reassuring words. Still, she couldn't completely chase away a slightly anxious feeling. She decided to do her best to ignore it. Today had been too much fun for some crazy stranger's wild ideas to ruin it. Stevie gave the saddle a last once-over with a rag and then stood up. "Come on, slowpokes. I'm starving."

"Me too," Lisa said. "It's time for TD's. Right, Mrs. Reg?"

Mrs. Reg peered at Lisa's saddle, then at Carole's, then Stevie's. All three were spotless, and the woman smiled. "Right," she told them. "Class dismissed. Have fun, girls."

A FEW MINUTES later The Saddle Club slid into their favorite booth at TD's. In honor of the fun they'd had at the rally, Stevie suggested they each order a sundae that matched the color of their horse. The waitress, who had walked up just in time to overhear, rolled her eyes but remained silent. She was used to Stevie's unusual ice-cream ideas.

Carole shrugged and grinned. "All right. In that case I'll have, um, chocolate ice cream with dark-chocolate sauce." Starlight was a bay—mahogany brown with a black mane and tail.

"What about his white star?" Stevie prodded.

Carole grinned. "Add a little whipped cream on top, please," she told the waitress.

"My turn," Lisa said. She thought for a second. "Okay, I think I'll have black cherry with chocolate sauce. That should match Prancer pretty well." She shrugged. "It would be more challenging if we didn't all ride bays," she remarked.

"You know, she's a bad influence on you girls," the waitress told Carole and Lisa, nodding at Stevie.

Stevie ignored the comment. "Okay, my turn," she said eagerly. "I'll have maple walnut ice cream—for No-Name's beautiful brown coat. Blackberry topping, for her mane and tail. And coconut sprinkles—lots of them—for her socks and exclamation point." She smiled proudly at the waitress. Carole and Lisa had the funniest feeling Stevie had been planning that particular order for some time.

The waitress just wrote it all down and walked away, shaking her head grimly. A few minutes later she returned with the sundaes. She dropped them on the table and hurried away without saying a word.

The girls dug into their sundaes with relish. "This is a perfect way to celebrate a perfect day," Carole declared through a mouthful of ice cream.

"Definitely," Lisa replied. "The rally was a lot of fun. I can't wait for the rematch next week."

"Me, too," Stevie said. She paused. "Do you think that girl will be there?"

The others immediately knew exactly who she meant. "Don't worry, Stevie," Carole said. "You heard Mrs. Reg. That girl is just mixed up."

"Mixed up, or crazy," Stevie corrected. "Or a horse thief who wants to get her hands on my horse."

"There's one other possibility," Lisa said slowly. "This girl at school once told me about a friend of hers who had a horse. She went on vacation once, and when she got back, she found out that her father had sold her horse while she was away."

Carole and Stevie gasped.

"How awful!" Carole exclaimed. She knew that her own father would never do such a thing. In fact, he was the one who had bought Starlight for her as a surprise Christmas present. Colonel Hanson knew very well how much Carole loved Starlight. He would never in a million years do something as rotten as selling the gelding behind her back. Still, it was scary even to think about it. "What happened?"

"She was so furious that she kicked and screamed until her father agreed to try to buy the horse back," Lisa explained. "But when he went back to the guy he'd sold it to, the guy told him he'd already resold the horse. And he didn't know where it had gone."

"I guess that could have happened," Carole said. "No-Name was one of a group of horses that Mr. Baker bought, right, Stevie?"

"Right," Stevie agreed. She put down her spoon, her face turning white. She had been dismissing the girl's claims as totally ridiculous. But now her friends seemed to be coming up with a lot of possible explanations that could mean they were true. "But that kind of thing probably doesn't happen very often," she said.

"I'm sure you're right about that. And it's not like No-Name is a Thoroughbred with a lip tattoo that can be easily checked," Lisa pointed out. "It could be hard to figure out if she's really that girl's horse. I mean, even if it were the same kind of situation."

"Which we definitely don't know that it is," Carole added, hoping to make Stevie feel better. "It seems pretty farfetched."

Stevie shook her head. "Even if it is, and even if No-Name is the right horse, there's no way I'd sell her back to that girl," she declared. "No way at all. No-Name is *my* horse, and that's that. End of story."

Before the others could answer, the little bell above the door tinkled and Veronica walked into the restaurant. She spotted them immediately and came over to the booth. "Hi there, teammates," she said. "Pretty good rally today, huh?"

"It sure was," Carole replied. She noticed that Veronica's brown hair had some new lighter streaks in it that hadn't been there earlier that day. "Did you just come from the hairdresser?" she guessed.

"Yes," Veronica confirmed, running a hand through her hair. "I figured I'd get some highlights to celebrate our near-victory. It was expensive, but I think it was worth it, don't you?"

"Sure," Carole said. She exchanged a furtive smile with her friends. So that was where Veronica had disappeared to after the rally when everybody else was at Pine Hollow working hard. It was just one more sign that Veronica hadn't changed her personality completely.

Veronica gestured at the seat beside Stevie. "Mind if I join you?" She didn't wait for an answer before sitting down—which was a good thing, because the other three girls were speechless with surprise. No matter how nice Veronica had been acting lately, none of them could believe that she would actually want to hang out with them outside the stable.

"So, what were you talking about?" Veronica asked, looking around the table.

"Um, not much," Stevie replied evasively.

Lisa could tell that her friend didn't want to share the real topic of their conversation with Veronica. She jumped to the rescue. "We were just talking about—about buying and selling horses," she explained quickly.

Veronica's face fell. She gulped and looked down at the table. "Oh," she said quietly, her eyes suddenly welling up with tears.

"What's the matter, Veronica?" Carole asked, astonished at the other girl's reaction. She couldn't imagine what had upset Veronica so much so quickly.

"Well," Veronica began. She gulped again and swiped at her eyes with her hand. "It's just, you know, Garnet and all—" She shrugged.

"What about Garnet?" Lisa prodded gently.

"It would just be really, well—it would hurt a lot to give up Garnet," Veronica said softly.

31

The others traded surprised glances. "Who says you have to give up Garnet?" Stevie asked.

But Veronica didn't answer. "I've got to go," she said, jumping up from the table. "I've got to, uh, catch the bus. I see it outside." She ran for the door.

The Saddle Club watched her go in surprised silence. Then Stevie found her voice. "You know what I said before about *Invasion of the Body Snatchers*? I take it back," she said. "Veronica is definitely possessed."

"I know what you mean," Carole said. "She really seemed upset at the thought of losing Garnet. I didn't know she could care about anything that much. Other than herself, I mean."

"Well, I didn't know she even knew what a public bus was, let alone that she'd ever consider taking one," Stevie said. "I doubt she's set foot on one in her whole life."

Lisa nodded. "This must mean that the rumors about the diAngelos' financial problems are true," she pointed out. "Why else would Veronica have to get rid of Garnet? Her parents must be talking about selling her."

"Well, that would definitely explain her reaction," Carole said. "I can't say I approve of the way Veronica takes care of Garnet—"

"*Doesn't* take care of her, you mean," Stevie interrupted.

"Exactly." Carole nodded. "Still, it would be tough on anyone to have to sell their horse."

32

"Anybody human, you mean," Stevie corrected. "I'm not sure Veronica qualifies."

"It's true," Lisa said. "Even though she's been ten times better lately, helping on the team and all, I still can't help remembering all the rotten things she's said and done up until now."

"I know what you both mean," Carole said. "But just now I really had the feeling she cared—a *lot*—about keeping Garnet. And I don't think it was just because she's the most expensive horse in the stable, either." She shook her head. "I think we need to give your body-snatcher theory some serious thought, Stevie."

The girls finished their ice cream in silence, doing just that.

4

AFTER RIDING CLASS the following Tuesday, Stevie, Carole, Lisa, and Veronica remained in the ring. They had arranged with Max to use the ring to practice their mounted games skills. Stevie still hadn't forgotten about Horse Wise's loss to Cross County at Saturday's rally. She was determined not to let the same thing happen at the rematch, and had gotten her teammates to agree to work extra hard to prepare for the event.

"Okay, what should we do first?" Lisa said when the rest of the class had left the ring.

Stevie thought for a second. "Well, we have no way of knowing exactly what games they'll throw at us on Saturday," she mused. "So I guess we should brush up on everything we possibly can before then so we'll be prepared for anything."

34

"Good idea," Carole said. "How about starting with the water race? Starlight and I had some trouble with that one the last time we tried it."

"Sounds good to me," Stevie said. "Let's get set up."

"I'll go get the water," Veronica volunteered. She dismounted, handing Garnet's reins to Carole, and hurried inside. A moment later she returned carrying a bucket, which she filled at the outside spigot near the door. Then she set the bucket, now brimming with water, on the barrel that Lisa had just dragged into the ring.

Veronica and Lisa remounted, and all four girls gathered on the far side of the ring.

"Ready?" Stevie asked. The others nodded. "Okay, I'll go first." She urged No-Name forward. The goal of this event was to race up to the bucket, pick it up, and ride back to the finish line without spilling any of the water. The first rider then handed the bucket to the second rider, who had to ride back and return it to the barrel. Then she rode back and the third rider started, and so on.

The mare's ears perked forward. She seemed to understand exactly what Stevie wanted. She cantered up to the barrel and came to a dead halt directly in front of it. Then she reached forward—and took a drink of water from the bucket.

"Hey!" Stevie exclaimed, surprised. A second later she started to laugh. When No-Name had slaked her thirst, Stevie picked up the lightened bucket and rode back at a trot to rejoin the others, who were doubled over with laughter. Stevie handed the bucket to Lisa. "Here you go," Stevie said, deadpan. "We didn't spill any."

That made the other girls laugh even harder, because Stevie was absolutely right. Still, they had a feeling the judges at the rally might not agree with the interpretation!

After that, the practice proceeded smoothly. All four riders did as well as they'd ever done at all the games. Stevie and No-Name, especially, were unbeatable. The mare seemed to understand all the games—and more than that, to enjoy them. When Stevie was putting on a jacket to simulate a costume for the costume relay, No-Name actually grabbed at the jacket with her mouth as if helping Stevie pull it on. In another horse, Stevie would have worried about encouraging nipping by letting her do it. But in No-Name it was clearly part of the spirit of the game. She just wanted to help. Stevie was bursting with pride in her horse by the time they decided to call it quits.

"Good practice, everyone," Carole declared as they headed inside.

"Absolutely," Veronica agreed cheerfully. "We're a shoo-in to win on Saturday." She glanced at her watch. "Whoops, I'd better hurry. My mother is picking me up in fifteen minutes."

Stevie, Carole, and Lisa glanced at one another. If Veronica was in a hurry, that meant she'd have to move quickly to take care of Garnet. And for Veronica, that usually meant moving quickly to wherever Red was and demanding that he take care of the horse for her.

But Veronica was still full of surprises. She managed to untack and groom Garnet, and even carry her tack to the tack room, before her mother arrived.

"See you guys tomorrow," Veronica called as she climbed into her mother's Mercedes. "And I'll try to remember to bring along a lid for that bucket so No-Name can't cheat again!"

The others laughed and waved. As the car pulled away, they walked back into the stable to clean their tack.

Carole shook her head. "Did you guys ever think we'd be joking around with Veronica diAngelo?" she asked.

"No way," Stevie replied. "Veronica almost seems human."

Lisa glanced around as they entered the tack room. Her gaze fell on a sweat-stained saddle that had been dropped carelessly onto its rack. "Well, don't get too excited about it yet," she said dryly. "She still isn't human enough to clean her own tack."

A HALF HOUR later Stevie was walking home through the fields beside the road, whistling cheerfully. She was pleased with the way the practice had gone, and especially about No-Name's part in it. Stevie had given her horse an extra ration of carrots to reward her for her trick in the water

37

race. One of the things Stevie loved most about No-Name was the horse's sense of humor. But then again, there really wasn't anything much about the mare that Stevie *didn't* love.

The fact that Veronica had continued to act like a normal person, even joking around with them, made Stevie feel even better. Stevie wondered if Mr. diAngelo's downfall was going to mean a permanent improvement in his daughter's personality. What a thought!

Stevie was still whistling as she reached her house. It was almost dinnertime, so she hurried upstairs for a quick shower, arriving back in the kitchen just as the rest of the family was sitting down around the table. Everyone looked up as she entered.

"Sorry I'm late," she said, sliding into her seat. She waited for some kind of rude comment from one of her brothers, but none of them said a thing. That was strange. Usually the three boys couldn't stop teasing her when Pine Hollow made her late for dinner. In fact, usually they couldn't stop teasing her at all.

Stevie glanced around. Her three brothers stared back at her solemnly. Stevie couldn't read their expressions. "What's wrong with everybody?" she demanded.

Her father cleared his throat. Stevie looked at him. "Well, Stevie," Mr. Lake began. He cleared his throat again. "We received a letter today—"

"Oh, is that what this is about?" Stevie interrupted before he could go any further. She took a deep breath. "I had a feeling my gym teacher would tell you. But you have to hear my side of the story. See, I only made that red inkstain on my gym uniform so I wouldn't have to do Modern Dance. I hoped she'd think I was bleeding from a serious cut and let me out. And you have to admit, Modern Dance is hardly the kind of thing we should be doing in gym class. It's not like playing softball or basketball or . . ."

Stevie's voice trailed off. Judging by the puzzled looks on her parents' faces, she had a sudden sinking feeling that that wasn't what they were going to say at all.

She swallowed hard. "What were you going to say, Dad?"

Her father glanced at Mrs. Lake before continuing. "Actually, Stevie, the letter is from a Mr. Anthony Webber. His daughter, Chelsea, is the owner of a bay mare, half Arabian and half Saddlebred, with uneven socks, long on the left, short on the right, and a stripe and a snip that resemble an upside-down exclamation point. The horse is named Punctuation for the exclamation point—Punk for short."

Stevie gasped. As hard as she had tried since the rally to forget about the blond girl, she hadn't quite been able to put the girl's outrageous claim out of her mind. Now every bit of worry she'd felt over the past few days came rushing back at once. How could this be happening? What did it mean?

With an almost superhuman effort, she managed to remain quiet and wait for her father to continue.

Mr. Lake had slipped into his lawyer voice by this time. "Several months ago," he continued, "Punk was stolen from the Webbers' barn. The family offered a thousand-dollar reward for anyone supplying information leading to the recovery of the mare, but no one came forward. Then, at the rally, Chelsea spotted No-Name. You, Stevie, appear to be the new owner of a horse who very much resembles Chelsea's Punk."

"She's my horse!" Stevie exclaimed. "What is this girl talking about?"

Her father looked back down at the letter. "Mr. Webber has assured me that there will be no need to involve the police if you simply return the horse to Chelsea."

"But—but—" Stevie spluttered, her face growing red. "I didn't steal her!"

"We know that, dear," Mrs. Lake said soothingly. "We know very well that you didn't do it."

"Just calm down, honey," Mr. Lake told Stevie, who was gripping the edge of the table so hard her knuckles were white. "Of course you had nothing to do with Punk's abduction—even if she and No-Name are the same horse, which hasn't been proven yet."

"That's right," agreed Mrs. Lake.

"In the meantime, your mother and I will do everything we can to get this issue settled as soon as possible," Mr. Lake assured his daughter.

Stevie's stomach tightened into a knot. She had the feeling that she was trapped in some kind of horrible nightmare. But when she pinched herself—hard—nothing happened. The only bit of consolation she could find was the fact that both her parents were lawyers. They dealt with this kind of thing every day. Surely they could stop the Webbers from going any further.

Suddenly another horrible possibility occurred to her. "What if this—this Chelsea person—goes and takes No-Name back?" she asked.

"Now that *would* be stealing," Mrs. Lake told her. "Until it's proven beyond a reasonable doubt that No-Name is Punk, the Webbers have no legal right to do that. No-Name is yours until proven otherwise."

"You mean if it's proven that she's the same horse, that girl will get her back?" Stevie asked, more horrified than ever.

Her parents exchanged a glance.

"Well, yes," Mrs. Lake admitted. "If they proved their case, by law, the horse would still be theirs. But that's a pretty big 'if' at this point."

"We have had no reason to believe up until this time that No-Name was ever stolen from anyone," Mr. Lake added. "The Webbers will need real, substantial proof. A lot of horses look alike, but that's not enough to prove they're the same horse."

Mrs. Lake nodded. "It'll be pretty tough for them to prove that No-Name is theirs, honey. Let's try not to worry until we know there's real cause for alarm." She grinned. "In the meantime you should be more concerned about the consequences of the inkstain incident."

Mr. Lake and the boys laughed.

"Good move, Stevie," Michael said.

But Stevie didn't have the heart to join in her family's laughter. Instead she rested her head in her hands. Her mind was spinning. A few minutes ago she had been perfectly happy, thinking about how well she and No-Name got along together, and how perfectly they were matched. And now she didn't know if she would ever ride her again!

Since Stevie had begun riding years ago, she'd been on the backs of a lot of horses and loved each and every one of them. But none of them, not even Topside, the Thoroughbred gelding at Pine Hollow whom Stevie adored, came close to No-Name in her heart. No-Name was special and she belonged to Stevie.

Stevie would never accept that No-Name was owned by someone else—even if it turned out to be true. She and the mare were destined to be together—forever. No law could ever change that.

WHEN STEVIE ARRIVED at Pine Hollow the next afternoon, she headed straight for No-Name's stall. Lisa and Carole found her there a few minutes later, talking softly to the mare. After dinner the night before, Stevie had called Carole and Lisa on three-way calling to tell them about the letter from Chelsea Webber's father. Then she had called Phil, then Carole again, then Lisa again, then Carole and Lisa together.

"There you are, Stevie," Carole cried, letting herself into the stall. She gave Stevie a hug. Next she gave No-Name a hug. The horse tossed her head and snorted, then started nibbling on Carole's curly black hair. "I couldn't sleep last night thinking about you and No-Name!"

"Me either," Lisa chimed in.

"Thanks, guys," Stevie replied. She opened the door and the three friends left the stall. "I almost wish I'd had the same problem. I kept having all these horrible dreams about being on the witness stand with dozens of lawyers shouting questions at me about No-Name." She shuddered. "In the end they all started accusing me of stealing her. Then the jury declared me guilty of 'grand theft, horse.'"

"Really? That's terrible," Lisa said.

"You're not kidding," Stevie said. "Hey, you guys were there, too. You were sitting with my parents in the audience."

"If your parents were watching, who was your lawyer?" Carole asked.

Stevie frowned. "Actually, I think it was Simon Atherton."

Her friends laughed. "No wonder you lost the case," Carole said. Simon was in the girls' riding class, but he wasn't a very good rider. He was enthusiastic about riding—and just about everything else—but that never quite seemed to help him get any better at it.

Stevie nodded thoughtfully. "Some of the people from Pine Hollow were in the jury, too," she said. "Meg and Betsy and Veronica and Adam and . . . I forget who else." She shook her head. "I can't believe they decided against me! They betrayed me!"

"Stevie, it *was* just a dream," Carole reminded her with a smile. Then her smile faded. "I can't believe the rest of it isn't a dream, too. Or a nightmare. I can't believe anyone would try to take your horse away."

Lisa nodded. "Me, neither. How are you holding up, Stevie?"

"I'm okay," Stevie said. "But I wish I'd never gone to that rally last weekend and bumped into Chelsea Webber. All of this would have never happened. I mean, obviously No-Name is my horse, not hers. It's all just a big mistake. So why does she have to drag me into her problems?"

Lisa shrugged. "You're right. You and No-Name were made for each other."

As if to prove Lisa's point, No-Name reached over the half door of her stall and grabbed at Carole's hair again. Then she swung her head around to nuzzle Stevie, as if to ask what she was doing out in the aisle.

Carole laughed. "See? Even No-Name agrees."

Just then Veronica came hurrying over. "Ready to get started?" she asked.

The others exchanged glances. Stevie took a deep breath. She knew there was no way she'd be able to keep Veronica from guessing that something was going on. She might as well just tell her about it. "Veronica, something happened last night," she said, and proceeded to tell Veronica the whole story—the phone call, Chelsea's stolen horse, the reward, and the Webbers' request that Stevie hand over No-Name to them.

When she finished, Veronica frowned and shook her

head. "I can't believe it," she declared. "That Chelsea Webber is obviously a low-life rat."

"My thoughts exactly," Stevie said, feeling more friendly toward Veronica than she ever had before. After all, wasn't that what friends did—stick up for one another? Stevie almost smiled in spite of herself. She couldn't believe she was thinking of Veronica diAngelo as a friend. But right now the only enemy in her life was Chelsea Webber.

"Anyway, Stevie, I can really sympathize," Veronica went on. "After all, you and I have a special kinship now."

"You do?" Carole asked a little skeptically. "What exactly is that?"

"We both own Arabian mares," Veronica replied, as if it were the most obvious thing in the world. "I mean, Stevie's horse isn't a purebred like Garnet, but she must be at least half Arabian and that's pretty good."

Carole rolled her eyes, but Stevie still felt warmly toward the other girl. "I guess," she said.

"Anyway," Veronica went on, "this Chelsea Webber girl is obviously insecure—or maybe she's just stupid. In any case, she certainly doesn't have any class. You should just ignore her, Stevie. Your parents are lawyers, aren't they? They should be able to deal with this in no time."

"Right," Stevie said, feeling a little better about the whole situation. Veronica was right. Stevie had nothing to worry about. Her parents would take care of everything.

Lisa glanced at her watch. "Come on," she said. "We'd better get started if we want to get any practicing done today." The others knew she was right, so they hurried off in different directions to get ready.

A few minutes later they reconvened in the outdoor ring and began practicing mounting and unmounting quickly. That skill was particularly important in relay races, since about half the races at most rallies required riders to get out of the saddle as part of the race. It was a skill that came easier to younger and smaller riders, because most of them rode ponies. A pony was defined as a horse under 14.2 hands in height. That meant riders on ponies had an advantage getting into and out of the saddle because they started out closer to the ground.

As Stevie was flinging herself into No-Name's saddle for about the tenth time, she noticed some movement outside the fence. When she was settled comfortably on No-Name's back she glanced over, thinking that Max or Mrs. Reg or Max's fiancée, Deborah Hale, must have come over to watch their practice. But when she saw who was standing by the fence, she let out a gasp. Suddenly she started breathing faster, feeling as if she'd just been punched in the stomach.

"Carole—Lisa—" she stammered. "L-look over there!"

Her friends looked. When they saw what Stevie had seen, they gasped, too. They both recognized the blond girl standing by the fence. It was Chelsea Webber!

"What's she doing here?" Stevie demanded loudly, glaring at the blond girl. "Why is she watching me?"

"I don't know," Lisa said. She put a protective hand on Stevie's arm. "But we won't let her get near you—or No-Name."

"What are you guys talking about?" Veronica asked, trotting over. She followed the direction of the others' gaze, and her eyes narrowed. "Oh," she said slowly. "That's her, isn't it?"

"It sure is," Stevie replied. She stared at Chelsea, but Chelsea didn't meet her eye. Instead, she stared at No-Name, a hint of a smile on her face. It was as if the other girls weren't even there.

"I wonder what she's doing here?" Carole muttered angrily. "She's caused enough trouble already with her stupid accusations."

Stevie was embarrassed to realize that her hands had started shaking uncontrollably. Suddenly all she wanted was to get away from the blond girl's intense gaze. She didn't want Chelsea Webber staring at her horse anymore. "Can we get out of here?" she asked weakly.

Her friends understood immediately. "I think I'm suddenly in the mood for a nice long trail ride," Carole declared. "How about you, Lisa?"

Lisa nodded. "Let's go," she said grimly. "Coming, Veronica?"

"You guys go ahead," Veronica said, her gaze still trained

on Chelsea. "I have a few things to say to that girl first. I'll catch up to you in a minute."

Stevie didn't need to be told twice. She rode over to the gate, being careful not to look at Chelsea, who was standing only a few feet away. Stevie tried not to notice that her horse glanced at the blond girl and snorted. Carole dismounted and opened the gate so that Stevie could ride through. As soon as Stevie was outside, she urged No-Name into a canter and rode until she was in the middle of the next field, where she slowed and waited for her friends to catch up.

A short time later the three girls were entering the cool, dim woods beyond the fields, and Stevie had calmed down a little. "You know where I'd like to go right now?" she said.

"The place by the creek?" Lisa guessed immediately.

Stevie nodded. Even though the weather was too cold for wading, the cool spot by Willow Creek, the stream that had given the girls' hometown its name, was the most soothing spot any of them knew.

They reached the spot in a matter of minutes, dismounted, and sat down on the bank of the stream. For a while they just sat in silence, watching the cool water tumble past.

Then Stevie blew her breath out in a loud, angry sigh. "I can't believe she had the nerve to show up here," she said. "I mean, isn't it bad enough that she's causing all this trouble without her coming and rubbing it in in person?"

"I know," Lisa agreed. "It really is pretty rotten of her. I wonder what she wants."

"Have your parents checked with Mr. Baker about where he got No-Name?" Carole asked.

"They were going to call him today," Stevie said. "I guess I'll find out what he said when I get home."

"I still can't believe anyone could think No-Name might belong to someone else," Carole said softly. "She's so perfect for you."

Stevie nodded and rested her chin on her hand. "I know."

"Maybe there's something we can do," Carole suggested. "Something to prove that it's totally impossible that No-Name could be that girl's horse. Or maybe we could figure out what her motives are for wanting her."

"Good idea," Stevie said, sitting up straight. "She probably has some nasty plot up her sleeve. I'm sure we could find out where she lives—then we could spy on her and try to figure it out!" Stevie rubbed her hands together. "Either that, or we could interview people she knows—you know, her teachers, classmates, that kind of thing. Maybe we'll find out she's a dangerous psycho with a history of mental instability."

Lisa rolled her eyes. "I think we should probably wait to hear what Mr. Baker says," she said logically. "After all, if he can trace where he got No-Name, it will be no problem for your parents to disprove Chelsea Webber's claim. With no need for espionage."

"True," Stevie said. Lisa's words should have made her feel better, but they didn't. What if Mr. Baker couldn't prove where No-Name came from? What would happen then?

The conversation was interrupted by Veronica's arrival. "Oh, there you are," she said when she spotted them. She rode over and dismounted. "It's safe to go back now if you want. Chelsea Webber is gone. And I don't think she's likely to come back anytime soon."

"What did you say to her?" Carole asked curiously.

Veronica smiled. "Well, I basically just gave her a piece of my mind. I told her exactly what I thought of her, and her grubby little plan to get her hands on Stevie's horse. Oh yes, and then I threw in a few choice words about that hideous outfit she was wearing."

The others laughed, even Stevie. What Veronica had been doing was being the Veronica diAngelo they knew and hated, superior and snobbish enough to make the most determined visitor vanish. And for once, they appreciated every ounce of snottiness that Veronica had at her disposal.

Veronica started to laugh, too. "I do have a way with people, don't I?" she said. And that made the others laugh even harder.

51

6

WHEN STEVIE ARRIVED home she found both her parents waiting once again for her. And the looks on their faces told her the news couldn't be good.

"What is it?" she demanded, a cold hard knot settling into her stomach. She still hadn't quite recovered from her encounter with Chelsea at the stable. The other girl's sudden appearance had taken her off guard and left her feeling shaken and helpless. And Stevie didn't like feeling helpless, especially when it came to her horse. "What did Mr. Baker say?"

"Oh, yes, Mr. Baker," Mr. Lake said. "I did speak to him this morning. He bought No-Name with a group of horses, from an agent who got them from all different places. He's going to try to trace where she came from, and your mother

52

and I have started our own investigation as well. But these things take time, and No-Name's history could be difficult or even impossible to trace."

Stevie shrugged. "Oh. Is that all you found out?"

"Not quite," Mr. Lake said. He glanced at his wife.

"What is it?" Stevie demanded again, looking from one to the other. It wasn't like her parents to be so hesitant. She had a bad feeling about what was coming.

"Well, honey," Mrs. Lake began, "your father also spoke to Mr. Webber this afternoon. . . ." She glanced at her husband.

"That's right, Stevie," Mr. Lake said. He shook his head. "And try as I did, I couldn't persuade him that No-Name isn't Punk."

"But he has to prove that she *is* Punk, right?" Stevie said. "That's what you said last night."

"Indeed he does," Mrs. Lake replied grimly. "And he's taken steps to enable himself to do just that." She held up a couple of pieces of paper. They were very official-looking, covered with lots of typing.

Stevie swallowed hard. "What are those?" she asked in a tiny voice.

"This one is sort of the equivalent of a search warrant," her mother explained. "It will allow the Webbers to have a vet examine No-Name."

"Oh," Stevie said. That didn't sound too bad. After all, any vet who examined No-Name would surely tell the

Webbers that there was no way she could be the same horse as Punk. "What about that other one?"

Mrs. Lake cleared her throat and glanced at her husband. "This one is a temporary restraining order," she explained gently. "It forbids you to ride the horse until this matter is settled. And it specifies that No-Name must remain at Pine Hollow Stable until everything is adjudicated—settled by a judge."

Stevie was speechless for a moment. Then she found her voice. "What?" she cried. "How can they do that? It's not fair—she's my horse! They can't forbid me to ride her!"

"Honey . . ." Mrs. Lake began.

But Stevie wasn't listening. "I just don't understand why this girl is doing this!" she exclaimed, her voice shrill. "What does she want from me? Why would anyone want to stop me from riding my own horse?"

"Stevie, just calm down," Mrs. Lake said firmly. "Getting hysterical isn't going to solve anything."

"Yes, sweetheart," Mr. Lake added, placing a comforting hand on Stevie's shoulder. "We're doing everything we can to straighten this whole thing out. The best thing for you to do is just to abide by the restraining order until we've had a chance to do that."

Stevie's whole body felt numb. She could see her father's hand on her shoulder, but she couldn't feel it. Her mind felt numb, too. How could this be happening to her?

Then she started shaking. She had to be alone. She

grabbed the papers from her mother, turned, and ran upstairs to her room. She closed the door, lay down on her bed, and stared at the ceiling. Her whole body was trembling. She had never felt like this before—beyond screaming or crying or becoming hysterical. Just numb and shaking so hard she thought she'd never stop.

She tried to calm herself by thinking about No-Name. She had to stay strong and focused for the mare's sake. She had to fight the Webbers so she and No-Name could stay together, just as they were meant to. How could stupid old Chelsea Webber even begin to think that No-Name ever could have belonged to her? That was ridiculous. And it didn't matter one bit what some judge said. No-Name belonged to Stevie, heart and soul, and she always would. That was that. Stevie just had to find a way to keep No-Name no matter what. She couldn't take any chances on what the judge decided.

Finally Stevie stopped shaking. She put down the papers, which were wrinkled now where she'd been clutching them, and sat up to pick up the phone on her bedside table. Silently praising the person who'd invented three-way calling, she got Carole and Lisa on the phone and told them the news.

They were almost as shocked as Stevie had been. But as they kept repeating over and over how horrible it all was, Stevie's mind was already racing in another direction.

"Listen, I think I've got an idea," she said suddenly,

interrupting Carole's string of insults against Chelsea Webber.

"What?" Lisa asked.

"How is anybody going to know whether I ride No-Name or not?" Stevie asked. "And how could anybody care? Nobody at Pine Hollow is going to turn me in to the Webbers, right? I can just keep on riding her anyway."

"That's right," Carole said excitedly. "After all, No-Name has to be exercised or she'll stiffen up. Even the stupid Webbers wouldn't want that to happen."

"Uh, hold on just a minute," Lisa put in. "I'm not sure that's such a good idea, Stevie. For one thing, Chelsea or her parents could turn up at Pine Hollow any old time— like she did today, for instance. Also, you've got to remember that you're dealing with legal documents and stuff here. And I'm pretty sure that violating court orders like that could land you in jail."

"Jail?" Stevie repeated. "Just for riding a horse?"

"Yes, just for riding a horse," Lisa replied. "Oops, there's my mom. I have to go eat dinner. Call me later if anything else happens, okay?"

Stevie promised to do so. Then she and Carole talked for a few more minutes until Carole, too, had to go downstairs for dinner.

After Stevie hung up the phone, she sat on the edge of her bed, thinking hard. She thought about what Lisa had said—that she might be thrown in jail just for riding her own horse. It didn't seem fair at all.

Then the answer came to Stevie. It was so simple she couldn't believe she hadn't thought of it before. She could only get in trouble for riding No-Name if anyone saw her doing it. But the Webbers couldn't possibly see her if she only rode inside. Stevie would have to convince Carole, Lisa, and Veronica to do all their practicing in the indoor ring. Then she'd just have to hope that the whole business was settled by Saturday so she could ride her horse in the Pony Club rally.

Stevie smiled for the first time since she'd arrived home that afternoon. It was so simple, it was brilliant—like the best of her schemes. Why hadn't she thought of it sooner?

There was a knock on her bedroom door. "Come in," Stevie called.

Her mother poked her head into the room. "Hi, sweetheart. I just wanted to see how you're holding up."

"I'm okay, Mom," Stevie assured her. "Really. It's all going to be okay."

"Well, I certainly hope so," Mrs. Lake said. "And I want you to know that your father and I are going to do absolutely everything we can to be sure you get to keep No-Name."

"I know, Mom," Stevie said. "I've never been more glad that you and Dad are both lawyers. And such good ones."

"Well, thanks, dear," her mother replied. "But remember, even good lawyers have to follow the rules. We have to obey the restraining order. So just in case you were cooking up one of your schemes to get around it by riding indoors or something like that, you should forget about it."

Stevie gasped. Her mother had read her mind.

"But Mom," she wailed. "I don't know if I can go for even a few days without riding No-Name! I just can't!"

"Well, you'll have to," Mrs. Lake said gently. "I'm sorry, but that's the way it has to be. We'll be here to help you through this, honey. Just hang in there."

"I'll try," Stevie muttered, but her heart wasn't in it.

"That's the spirit," Mrs. Lake said. "Why don't you come on downstairs now? Dinner will be ready in a few minutes."

"I'll be right down," Stevie replied. After her mother left, Stevie sat on the edge of her bed for a minute, staring into space. She was still having trouble believing that she was actually forbidden to ride her horse.

Then another thought crept into her mind. How had her mother guessed her plan so fast? She wondered if either of her parents had ever been as sneaky and clever as she was. They must have been, since they'd figured out exactly what was on her mind.

Stevie almost smiled. Somehow the thought made her feel just a tiny bit better. She got up and headed downstairs for dinner.

THE NEXT DAY after school Stevie, Carole, and Lisa met at Pine Hollow to practice for the rally. Even though Stevie wasn't going to be able to ride No-Name, they still wanted to be prepared. After all, the rally was two whole days away. It was possible that everything would be cleared up by then so that No-Name could compete.

Veronica was nowhere in sight. The girls went to Garnet's stall to check there, but the mare was alone.

"Where could she be?" Carole wondered.

Stevie shrugged. "She didn't mention anything to me today in school about not coming." Stevie and Veronica were students at Fenton Hall, a private school on the other side of town from the public school that Carole and Lisa attended.

"Oh, well," Lisa said with a shrug. "We'll just have to get started without her, I guess."

"I can't say I'm sorry about that," Carole remarked. "Even if she has been nice lately."

"Come on," Stevie said. "Let's go ask Mrs. Reg if it's okay for me to ride Topside today." She shook her head. "I still can't believe my parents figured out what I was up to."

Carole grinned. "Sneakiness is in your genes, Stevie."

"Maybe that's why your parents are such good lawyers," Lisa chimed in.

"That's my theory, too," Stevie agreed.

They found Mrs. Reg in her office off the tack room. "Hello, girls," she greeted them. "I'm glad you're here. I have a message for you from the fourth member of your team."

"You mean Veronica?" Carole asked. "We were wondering what happened to her. What's the message?"

"She won't be able to make it today. She's at the car dealership with her mother," Mrs. Reg explained.

"The car dealership?" Stevie repeated. "Don't tell me they're getting her her own chauffeur-driven Mercedes."

Mrs. Reg shook her head. "Quite the contrary. Mrs. diAngelo wanted Veronica to come along to the Ford dealership. They're trading in their Mercedes for a Ford."

"A Ford?" the three girls exclaimed in one voice. They all tried to picture snobbish, stylish Mrs. diAngelo behind the wheel of such an inexpensive car. They couldn't do it.

"That's right," Mrs. Reg said. "Veronica was careful to explain that after the snow we had this winter, her parents thought a Ford would be able to handle the roads better."

"Yeah, right," Stevie said skeptically.

"We've heard all kinds of rumors about Mr. diAngelo's losing his job," Carole told Mrs. Reg. "Do you know what the real story is?"

Mrs. Reg scratched her chin thoughtfully. "Well, girls, I probably shouldn't be talking to you about this, but I know you and Veronica have been spending quite a bit of time together, so you might as well know. She might be needing some friends pretty soon."

"What is it, Mrs. Reg?" Lisa asked.

"Well, I don't know all the details," Mrs. Reg said, "but it seems that some important papers are missing down at Mr. diAngelo's bank."

"What kind of papers?" Carole asked.

"That I couldn't tell you," Mrs. Reg said with a shrug. "But apparently they're important enough to mean that the bank might have to shut down if they're not found soon. And if that happens, Mr. diAngelo will surely be bankrupt. Most of his assets are tied up in that bank."

The girls exchanged glances.

"That's terrible," Carole said, speaking for all of them. Even though they had joked about it before, the girls knew that it would be a serious thing if Mr. diAngelo really did lose his job.

"Yes, it is," Mrs. Reg agreed. "The family would have to sell whatever they could to raise cash. They might even have to sell their home. And Mr. diAngelo has already spoken to Max about trying to find a buyer for Garnet."

Stevie, Carole, and Lisa exchanged another glance.

"So we were right. That's why she was so upset the other day at TD's," Lisa said.

"But do you think they'll really have to sell Garnet?" Carole asked Mrs. Reg.

"I don't know," she answered. "I also don't know if Max and I will be able to help find a buyer. We're not really used to dealing with horses as valuable as Garnet. But Max knows a few people farther downstate who might be interested."

Carole shook her head. It was too horrible to think about. Now not only Stevie, but Veronica, too, might actually lose her horse to a stranger! "How awful," was all she could manage to say.

"As I said, Veronica is going to need some friends to support her if the worst does happen," Mrs. Reg told them. "I know you girls haven't always gotten along in the past, but that seems to be changing. I hope you'll be there for her the way you always are for one another."

"We will," Carole assured her earnestly. "After all, she's been really supportive of Stevie this past week." Lisa and Stevie nodded.

"Oh, yes, that reminds me," Mrs. Reg said, turning to Stevie. "We received a copy of that restraining order yesterday. I'm very sorry, but we're going to have to enforce it strictly. Otherwise Max and I could get into a lot of legal trouble."

Stevie felt the blood rush to her face. "I understand," she said softly. "Does that mean I can't go anywhere near No-Name while I'm here?"

"Not at all," Mrs. Reg said. "In fact, we're counting on you to continue taking good care of the horse. The only things you're prohibited from doing are riding her and removing her from Pine Hollow."

"Oh," Stevie said, feeling a little better. It wasn't the same as riding, but she was glad to know that she'd at least be able to spend time with No-Name, talking to her and taking care of her and reminding her how much she loved her. And that was definitely better than nothing.

"Until this matter is settled, you're welcome to go back to riding Topside," Mrs. Reg said.

"Oh, thanks," Stevie said. "I was just going to ask about that."

The girls split up and Stevie decided a visit to No-Name would have to wait until after practice. She headed for Topside's stall with his tack. The big bay gelding greeted her affectionately. She gave him a hug and then quickly got him ready to go.

Her friends were waiting for her in the outdoor ring

when she arrived. Stevie led Topside into the ring and then mounted, giving herself a leg up on the fence.

It felt strange to be back in Topside's saddle again. Even in a few short weeks she had grown accustomed to No-Name—the way she moved, her height, and most of all, her distinctive personality.

Topside stood quietly, awaiting Stevie's signal. She was reminded of what a well-trained, intelligent horse he was. She sighed. Even if she couldn't ride No-Name in the rally on Saturday, maybe she'd at least still be able to beat Phil on Topside. She touched the horse lightly behind the girth with her heel, and he stepped off instantly. Stevie rode over to Carole and Lisa, who were in the midst of arguing about the best strategy for musical chairs.

"We're ready," Stevie announced as she joined them. "What should we do first?"

"Hmm." Carole thought for a second. "Why don't we work on the on-and-off obstacle race? Mr. Baker loves that one—he's sure to put it on the program on Saturday."

"Good idea," Lisa said.

The girls quickly readied a makeshift course. They arranged some empty barrels, sacks of grain, and other objects in the ring. They even dragged out a bale of hay, which they placed in the center. In this race, the judge laid out a complicated course over and through and around the various objects, which each rider had to follow carefully. The winner was the rider who was the most exact in following instructions. In the case of a tie, the prize went to the competitor with the fastest time.

"Okay," Carole said, dusting off her hands and surveying their handiwork. She quickly came up with a course and described it to her friends. "Now let's get started. Who wants to go first?"

"I will," Lisa volunteered. She mounted and signaled to Prancer. She moved off obediently at a walk. They completed the course easily, except when Prancer refused to step over the bale of hay. Finally Lisa had to give up and lead her around it instead.

When she returned to her friends at the end, she was frowning. "We'd lose a lot of points for that refusal," she said. "She's never done that before. What do you think is wrong?"

Carole shrugged. "You were doing everything right," she told Lisa. "Prancer must just be having a bad day. It happens. You have to remember, she's pretty new to this." Prancer had been bred and raised to be a racehorse, and she still wasn't completely used to everything Lisa asked her to do.

"I know," Lisa replied. "She's such a dream to ride most of the time that it's easy to forget that sometimes. Anyway, I hope she's better by Saturday." She scratched the horse behind the ears to show that she wasn't angry with her.

"Okay, my turn," Stevie announced. She started the course. Topside was alert and responsive as she directed

65

him around the first barrel. He didn't take a wrong step weaving in and out down a row of buckets.

She dismounted and led him toward the hay bale. His ears pricked forward when he saw it, and he started to turn aside to go around it. Stevie corrected him quickly, and he responded just as quickly, stepping forward straight toward the hay bale. Stevie hopped up onto it, urging Topside to step up. He looked a little puzzled, but obeyed, moving slowly and cautiously, lifting first one foreleg and then the other. Stevie praised him and hopped down on the other side. Topside shook his head a little, but then his years of careful training won out and he did as Stevie asked.

However, it was obvious that he hadn't liked it. When all four feet were safely on solid ground on the far side of the bale, Topside shook his head again and snorted, moving a few steps away from the hay bale. Stevie moved with him, speaking to him soothingly. When she was sure he was calm, she started to mount.

Unfortunately, she misjudged the location of the stirrup, and her foot missed its mark. Blushing furiously, she tried again and swung up easily into the saddle, mentally scolding herself. That was a beginner's mistake, and she shouldn't have made it. But she had been distracted by Topside's skittishness and had aimed for the stirrup without looking. Being used to No-Name, who was at least a hand shorter than Topside, she had missed.

The next few obstacles were relatively uneventful, although Topside hesitated a little before stepping over some bags of grain, obviously confused once again about what he was being asked to do.

The part of the course that Stevie was most worried about was the last part, which involved picking up a flag that Carole had set on a bucket, carrying it across the finish line, and planting it in the dirt. One reason Topside was at Pine Hollow now instead of still competing in the show ring was that he'd shied badly at a national horse show when someone in the crowd had waved a cape as he approached a jump. Stevie was afraid that a fluttering flag might spook him just as much.

When Stevie reached the barrel, she reached over and picked up the flag slowly and carefully, letting Topside see her do it. He watched calmly as it fluttered a little in the breeze, and she let out the breath she'd been holding. She urged him forward and finished the course, dismounting and jabbing the flagpole deep into the dusty ground.

Stevie was disappointed with the performance. She knew her time had been a lot slower than Lisa's. And even though Topside hadn't actually refused any of the obstacles, he had clearly been a little perplexed about the whole thing. He was a wonderful, spirited, talented horse, but he just didn't seem to understand this kind of game. He was a show horse, not a games horse. If only Stevie could be riding No-Name right now! The mischievous mare always

67

seemed to be enjoying mounted games just as much as her mischievous rider—if not more.

Stevie sighed with frustration, hoping the rest of the games would go better.

BY THE END of the practice session, Stevie's mood had gone from bad to worse. Topside had done his best, but it was clear to all of them that he just wasn't as good at the games as No-Name was.

Stevie gave him a good grooming and a few extra treats. "Sorry about that, Topside," she said, scratching him in his favorite spot. "You know and I know that you're tops when it comes to jumping and dressage. But I can tell you weren't having any fun out there just now. You were a good sport to put up with it."

She sighed as she let herself out of his stall. This was one more thing she could blame on Chelsea Webber. If Horse Wise suffered a humiliating defeat at the hands of Cross County on Saturday, it would be all her fault.

Stevie dropped Topside's tack in the tack room, making a mental promise to clean it later, and headed for No-Name's stall. At least now she would get to spend some time with her horse. Maybe that would cheer her up.

She found Lisa waiting outside the stall to help her, holding No-Name's grooming bucket. Carole was still working on Starlight's grooming in the stall next door.

"Here you go." Lisa handed the bucket to Stevie. "I'll go

help Carole finish up so you can have a few minutes alone. Then we'll come over and help."

"Thanks," Stevie said, grateful as always to have such understanding best friends. She entered the stall and greeted No-Name with a big hug. The mare seemed happy to see her, moving forward as if she expected to leave the stall.

"No, sorry, girl," Stevie told her, closing the half door behind her. "We can't go riding today." She set the grooming bucket in a corner of the stall and started to pick out the horse's hooves. No-Name turned her head and snuffled at Stevie's hair, then lowered her head to examine the grooming bucket. Stevie smiled at the mare's endless curiosity.

"I know you're bored and restless in here," she said. She put down the hoof pick and grabbed a dandy brush, running it down the mare's back and sides with brisk strokes. "I would be, too. It must be just like being grounded." She frowned at the thought.

Stevie could hear her friends chatting in the next stall, discussing ways to improve their performance on Saturday. But Stevie paid no attention. She knew that if she couldn't ride No-Name on Saturday, all the strategy in the world wouldn't help. Strategy and practice couldn't replace the innate ability that some horses had for mounted games. No-Name had that ability. Topside didn't. Even if they had a lot more time to practice, which they didn't, they wouldn't be able to make up for that—any more than spending more time grooming No-Name was going to be able to make up for not being able to ride her.

Stevie sighed. No-Name looked at her and snorted. A second later, the mare suddenly moved to the front of the stall and stuck her head out over the half door.

"We'll be right back, Stevie," Carole called. "We're just going to the tack room to drop off Starlight's stuff." Stevie heard two sets of footsteps moving off down the aisle. No-Name continued to look out the stall door for a moment, apparently watching them go. Then she stamped her feet and shifted her weight, swinging her head from side to side. She backed away from the door for a minute, then quickly moved back and looked out again.

"Just hold still for another second, okay?" Stevie said to No-Name, who seemed to be getting more and more restless. She ran a soft cloth over No-Name's body, then dropped it back in the bucket. No-Name looked perfect. Since she hadn't been out that day, grooming her hadn't taken very long. Stevie was trying to think of something else she could do to prolong their time together when she heard the mare snort loudly.

Stevie looked up. No-Name still had her head out the door, and now she seemed to be staring down the aisle at something. Stevie moved to the door next to the mare and looked out, expecting to see Carole and Lisa returning.

She gasped in shock when she saw who was walking

down the stable aisle toward her. It was Chelsea Webber!
Two men were with her, and Mrs. Reg was walking behind
them. The older of the two men was wearing a business suit
and had his arm slung protectively around the girl's shoulder. Stevie figured he must be Mr. Webber. The younger
man was dressed more casually and carrying an equipment
bag. Immediately Stevie guessed why they were here. This
was the vet who was going to try to determine No-Name's
true identity.

Stevie gulped. The anger that had been simmering inside her for the last several days seemed to gather steam.
How dare Chelsea do this to her! How dare she come to
Pine Hollow—the place Stevie loved most in the world—
to see No-Name, and bring a vet to examine her.

As the group drew closer, Mrs. Reg caught Stevie's eye
and gave her a warning glance, as if the older woman knew
how close Stevie was to losing it.

Before she did or said anything she would regret, Stevie
backed into the stall and stood protectively next to No-
Name. Maybe Chelsea was legally entitled to come here.
And maybe she was even legally entitled to bring her father and the vet. But one thing was for sure. Stevie would
never make it easy for the other girl.

8

CAROLE AND LISA were still chatting about the rally when they turned the corner to return to No-Name's stall. But when Carole saw the group of people standing around No-Name's stall, she stopped talking in midsentence. "What's going on?" she wondered. Then she spotted Chelsea and her eyes narrowed. "And what's *she* doing here?"

"I don't know," Lisa replied grimly. "But we'd better get over there and find out."

They hurried to the stall, arriving just in time to hear Mrs. Reg introduce Stevie to the vet whom the Webbers had brought to examine No-Name. Stevie was glowering furiously. Carole elbowed her way past the others to Stevie's side.

"You don't have to be here for this, Stevie," she told her

friend, putting her arm around Stevie's shoulders. She wasn't sure it was a good idea for Stevie and Chelsea to be together right now.

"That's right," Lisa said, joining them and shooting Chelsea a dirty look.

"Your friends are right, Stevie," Mrs. Reg told her quietly. "I'll be here to keep an eye on everything. You might want to head home."

But Stevie shook her head stubbornly. "She's my horse," she said between clenched teeth. "I want to be here for this. I want them to see what good care I've taken of *my horse*." She stressed the last two words, staring at Chelsea defiantly. The older girl didn't meet her gaze. She was staring at No-Name.

Mrs. Reg nodded. "All right, then. She stays." Mr. Webber started to say something, but Mrs. Reg cut him off with a curt, "And that's that."

Mr. Webber shrugged. "Fine. Let's get on with it," he said. He nodded to the vet, who entered the stall and began to examine No-Name. The mare stood quietly, gazing out at all the people gathered outside her stall.

After a moment the vet stuck his head out over the door. "Could someone bring a bucket of fresh water, please?" he said.

"I'll get it," Stevie said quickly and a little too loudly.

Chelsea frowned. "No, let me," she countered just as quickly.

73

"I said, *I'll* get it," Stevie insisted.

"And *I* said I want to do it!" Chelsea snapped back.

"I don't care who gets it," the vet said. "Actually, you could each bring one—I'll probably need two buckets anyway."

"You heard him, Stevie," Mrs. Reg said. "Why don't you show Chelsea where we keep the water buckets?"

"Fine." Stevie stalked off toward the equipment room, not even looking to see if Chelsea was following. She couldn't believe the way this girl was pushing her way into things, trying to take over. Wasn't it bad enough that she was trying to take away No-Name?

Chelsea hurried after Stevie. "She *is* my horse, you know," she said, sounding a bit tentative, as soon as they were out of earshot of the others.

"No she's not," Stevie said angrily. "She's mine and always will be." She tossed her head. "So you might as well give up on your pathetic attempts to get her away from me."

"She's *not* yours, and she never was," Chelsea snapped. "And our vet is back there right now proving it. It'll be a snap once he determines for sure that she's allergic to weeds." She gave Stevie a nasty smile. "And you for one know that she is. Weren't you the smart one who figured it out?"

Stevie gasped. Chelsea knew about No-Name's weed allergy! Stevie remembered how proud she'd been when she had figured out the cause of No-Name's allergic reactions. After No-Name had had several mysterious outbreaks of hives, Stevie had spotted the horse eating weeds and guessed they were the culprit. At the time Stevie had thought her detective work made her relationship with No-Name extra special and unique. But it looked as though Chelsea planned to use that against her. Stevie suddenly wished more than anything that she'd never even heard the word allergy before.

Chelsea continued to smile, obviously observing that she'd hit a nerve. "You see?" she said. "So you'd be better off saving your stupid insults for someone who deserves them. I'm just trying to get my horse back."

By this time they had reached the equipment room. Stevie grabbed two buckets and shoved one of them at Chelsea. "Here," she hissed. In silence, the two girls filled the buckets with water and headed back.

Chelsea started to whistle softly. Stevie gritted her teeth, hating the other girl more and more with every step.

When they reached the stall, Stevie set down the water bucket and then turned to face Chelsea, hands on her hips. "Just because you know about No-Name's allergy doesn't mean you've won," she said, fighting to keep her voice steady. But she could feel tears stinging her eyes and a sob creeping up into her throat. "No-Name and I are meant to be together. Even you should be able to see that." She turned away so Chelsea wouldn't see her wiping her eyes

75

on her sleeve. Stevie knew that Mrs. Reg had been right to urge her to go home. If she didn't leave within the next few seconds, she had a feeling she would just explode. "I have to get out of here," she whispered to Carole and Lisa.

They exchanged glances and nodded. "Let's go," they said in one voice. They each took one of Stevie's arms and started off.

Then Lisa stopped. "Oh! We never cleaned our tack. . . ." she began.

Mrs. Reg came forward, shaking her head and shooing them away. "You're too conscientious, Lisa," she said. "Get Stevie home. I'll take care of your tack this once."

"Thanks, Mrs. Reg," Carole called over her shoulder as they hurried away. "We owe you one!"

When the girls reached Stevie's house, Mr. and Mrs. Lake were waiting for them in the front hallway. "Mrs. Reg called to say you were coming," Mr. Lake said, taking Stevie into his arms for a hug.

Stevie sniffled as she hugged him back. "I couldn't stay there with them any longer, Dad," she said. "I wanted to stay for No-Name's sake, but I just couldn't."

"I know, sweetheart," he said soothingly. "It's okay. Come on inside and have a seat."

Mrs. Lake led them into the kitchen, where she had set out a plate of cookies. They all sat down around the table. Mr. Lake pushed the plate toward Stevie.

"I'm not hungry," she said, taking a cookie and shoving

it into her mouth. She couldn't stop thinking about what had happened back at the stable. She was burning with anger toward Chelsea Webber. And she was angry with herself, too, for not being able to stay with her horse. Instead, she'd run away again, just as she had when Chelsea had surprised her at the outdoor ring. But she was determined not to do it again. She would fight Chelsea, tooth and nail, to the bitter end. She would do anything to make sure she and No-Name could be together.

"Honey, you'll be glad to know I've had all my junior partners scouring the statute books all day on your behalf," Mrs. Lake said.

"Really?" Stevie said, taking another cookie. "Just the junior partners? Why didn't you have the senior partners help, too?"

"Because they were preparing the arguments for the judge," her mother replied. "Try not to worry, honey. We're doing everything we can. So is Mr. Baker. He's trying like crazy to figure out where No-Name came from. The only thing you can do is sit back and wait."

"But that's what I hate the most," Stevie said plaintively.

Mr. and Mrs. Lake nodded sympathetically. Carole and Lisa did, too.

Stevie's brothers came into the kitchen and joined them.

"Hi, Stevie," Alex said shyly. He nodded at Carole and

Lisa. None of the boys seemed to know what to say. Chad sat down and shoved two cookies into his mouth. The other boys just stood there, shifting their weight from foot to foot.

Just then the phone rang. Stevie jumped.

Mr. Lake got up and answered it. "Yes?" he said. "Oh, yes, hello."

By the expression on her father's face, Stevie could tell it was about No-Name. She held her breath.

"I see," Mr. Lake said into the phone. "Yes. I see. Yes, I recall. Mmm-hmm. Well, all right then. We'll be in touch. Of course. Yes. Good-bye."

He hung up, and Stevie jumped out of her chair and hurried over to him. "Who was that?" she asked anxiously.

Mr. Lake ran one hand through his hair. "That was the Webbers' lawyer," he said. He walked over to the table and sat down. "Have a seat, Stevie."

STEVIE DID AS her father said, and sat down, but it was as if someone else were going through the motion. When she looked back at her father her head felt thick and foggy. Maybe she was dreaming or sleepwalking. This couldn't be real. It couldn't be happening to her.

Stevie barely paid attention when Carole spoke up. "What did he say, Mr. Lake?" she asked. "Was the lawyer calling about the vet's visit?"

Mr. Lake nodded. He stared at Stevie, a serious look on his face. "After the preliminary results from the vet, it looks as though No-Name and Punk are indeed one and the same horse."

"Oh, Stevie," Carole whispered, taking her friend's hand.

Stevie didn't even seem to notice the comforting gesture. Her face had turned white and she stared at her father. She gripped the edge of the table. "Why are they so sure?" she asked.

Mr. Lake sighed. "Several reasons," he said. "For one thing, No-Name's markings are rather unusual. . . ."

"But that's not enough proof!" Stevie cried. "You said it yourself. They need more evidence than that!"

"Stevie," Mrs. Lake said quietly, "let your father finish."

"Yes, Stevie, there is more evidence," Mr. Lake said. "Not only does No-Name resemble Punk exactly, but there's also the matter of the identical weed allergies."

Stevie groaned. "I can't believe I ever boasted about figuring that out," she said miserably, burying her head in her arms.

"That doesn't matter, Stevie," Mrs. Lake reassured her. "The vet would have known to check for it anyway."

"The other major piece of evidence," Mr. Lake continued, "is the bone splint."

Stevie looked up, and her eyes widened. Pine Hollow's vet, Judy Barker, had declared No-Name's bone splint perfectly harmless before the Lakes had bought the mare. "You mean Punk had the same thing?"

"That's right," her father said. "The Webbers' vet just re-X-rayed it. It's identical."

"So No-Name's real name is Punctuation Webber," Stevie said. She felt tears welling up uncontrollably, but she didn't care. She couldn't fight the facts—or the law. "I have to go see her!" she wailed. "I have to say good-bye to her one last time!" She jumped out of her seat.

"Stevie, calm down," Mrs. Lake said, grabbing her arm and gently pulling her back down. "I admit, the proof does seem rather conclusive, but it has to be approved by the court before the Webbers can reclaim the horse."

"Your mother's right," Mr. Lake agreed. "And that can't possibly happen before next week, so you'll have No-Name at least until then. You'll have plenty of time to say good-bye."

Stevie nodded, too brokenhearted to answer. She knew one reason she would be at Pine Hollow between now and next week—the rally. She had been looking forward to it so much. But now it was ruined. She wouldn't be able to ride No-Name—*her* horse. Not in the rally. Not ever again.

Never. The unspoken word echoed in her ears. Never.

WHEN STEVIE ARRIVED at Pine Hollow after school the next day, the first person she saw was Veronica diAngelo. Almost before she realized it, Stevie had blurted out the whole story to her.

Veronica was sympathetic. "I know exactly how you feel," she told Stevie. "I know just how much you can love your horse, and how much it hurts when you know someone is trying to take her away. It's how I feel about Garnet."

Stevie nodded. She'd been so caught up in her own problems for the past few days that she'd forgotten all about Veronica's. She felt a little guilty about it, especially now that Veronica was being so understanding about No-Name. "I've been meaning to tell you that I'm sorry about what you and your family are going through," she said, feeling a little awkward.

Veronica shrugged. "Yeah, it's a bummer," she said quietly, staring at the ground.

"I know you've always . . . well, that you've gotten used to living a certain way," Stevie said, thinking of the diAngelos" huge house, swimming pool, and servants—not to mention Veronica's designer wardrobe, and of course, Garnet. "I guess if your dad really does lose his job it'll be hard to do without all that."

Veronica gasped.

"Sorry," Stevie said quickly, ashamed of her tactlessness. "I guess I shouldn't have just come right out about your father's job like that."

"No, it's not that," Veronica said, biting her lip. "It's not your fault, anyway. It's just the thought of doing without. I'm not really used to it yet."

"I know what you mean," Stevie said. "I'm definitely not used to the idea of losing No-Name yet, even though I know it's true." She frowned at the thought. She'd lain awake all night trying to think of ways to keep No-Name —everything from training the mare to bite Chelsea on command to convincing the judge that Stevie would waste away to nothing without her. At about three A.M. Stevie had even considering stealing No-Name away from Pine Hollow in the dead of night and hiding her in Phil's barn. But she soon realized that Mr. and Mrs. Marsten probably wouldn't go along with that. And hiding the mare in the woods wouldn't work, either. The nights were still too chilly, and besides, someone was bound to find her sooner or later. Finally, as the first rays of sunlight had started peeking through her bedroom window, Stevie had admitted defeat. And that was the hardest thing she'd ever done in her life.

Veronica nodded. "I've had a lot longer than you've had to get used to the thought of losing my horse," she said, beginning to sniffle a little. "And I'm not used to it, either."

"I guess we have more in common now than we ever thought we would, huh?" Stevie said sadly. "We're both losing something that's really important to us."

Veronica nodded again. Her sniffles were turning to full-fledged tears now. "Y-you're the only one who really understands, S-Stevie," she gasped between sobs. "Wouldn't it be funny if you wound up buying Garnet?" The thought of this seemed to upset her all over again. She broke out into fresh sobs.

Almost without thinking about it, Stevie reached out to give the other girl a comforting hug. As Veronica sobbed on her shoulder, Stevie couldn't help thinking that, right at this moment, the spoiled rich girl felt almost like a real friend.

Carole and Lisa arrived just then and found them. They were both a little surprised at the scene, but did their best not to show it. When Veronica saw them, she immediately wiped away her tears.

"Ready to start practice, you two?" Carole asked, trying to sound as cheerful as possible under the circumstances.

Stevie nodded. She decided she'd swing by No-Name's stall for a quick hello, then spend some quality time with her after the practice.

A few minutes later the four girls met up again in the outdoor ring. Stevie was riding Topside once again.

"All right, how about starting with the two-handed water balloon race?" Carole said. She was leading Starlight and carrying a bucket full of water balloons, which she'd just filled.

The others agreed, and they got started. Carole set the bucket at one side of the ring. Then she mounted and tied Starlight's reins together. This race was partly a test of balance and partly a test of the rider's skill in using aids other than the reins to control her horse. As soon as Carole was settled in the saddle Lisa handed her two very full water balloons—the race was also partly a test of a rider's skill in holding on to two slippery water balloons and passing them off to her teammates without dropping or breaking them.

Carole managed to ride Starlight across the ring without too much trouble. She'd been working hard with him on responding to leg aids, and he had learned his lessons well. Still, she kept him at a walk this time.

Stevie was waiting to take the balloons from Carole. Then she urged Topside forward, aiming him across the ring to where Lisa was waiting. The gelding responded immediately, moving into a smooth walk. At times like this, Stevie was reminded once again of Topside's former life as a champion show horse, who had been trained since birth to obey his rider's every command.

When they were halfway across the ring, Stevie decided to try a trot. Once again, Topside was paying perfect attention, and he responded instantly to her signal. But Stevie wasn't as ready for the change in gaits as she thought she was. Without realizing it, she'd been expecting No-Name's distinctive bouncy trot. Topside's gait was different, and it threw her off balance. In the split second it took her to regain it, one of the water balloons managed to wriggle its way out of her grasp. It slipped forward, bursting onto Topside's neck and spraying water all over the horse and his rider.

Topside, startled, shook his head violently and came to a full stop, almost unseating Stevie once again. She tossed the other water balloon aside and grabbed the reins, quickly regaining control of her mount. She patted and talked soothingly to the gelding for a minute, until he seemed to calm down.

But the soaking had thrown Topside off, and he continued to shake his head nervously as Stevie rode him back toward the bucket. "I don't think Topside likes this one," Stevie called to her friends. "Maybe we should practice something else for a while."

The others nodded. They didn't say anything, but Stevie suspected they were thinking the same thing she was, which was that Topside just didn't seem to like any of the mounted games as much as No-Name did. Stevie couldn't help comparing the gelding's reaction to the water balloon with No-Name's active participation in the water race a few days earlier. She also remembered how, at a practice the week before, she'd slipped and dropped both water balloons on the mare. No-Name had seemed a little surprised at the unexpected shower, but it hadn't fazed her for more than a few seconds.

No-Name is such a great horse, Stevie thought with a sigh. The familiar wave of sadness swept over her. She couldn't bear the thought of not riding the mare in the rally tomorrow—not to mention losing her forever. If only she could ride the horse one more time. Maybe that would make saying good-bye just a little bit easier.

Stevie watched as Veronica dismounted and removed

her hard hat, shaking out her long hair. "Well, what should we do next?" she asked.

Stevie froze, watching the highlights in Veronica's hair shimmer in the sun. "That's it!" she cried.

"What's what?" Lisa asked.

"Veronica just gave me a great idea," Stevie said. "Actually, her highlights gave me the idea. Remember when I gave you a makeover, Lisa?"

Lisa nodded and rolled her eyes. The experiment hadn't been very successful. Stevie had borrowed all of Mrs. Atwood's makeup—and had managed to get just about all of it on Lisa's face. It had taken Lisa twenty minutes to scrub it all off—which she'd done as soon as she'd looked in the mirror.

"I remember," Carole said with a giggle. "I especially remember the look on Lisa's face—what you could see of it under all that makeup, that is—when you said you wanted to dye her hair."

Stevie grinned. "That's exactly it," she said. "That's how I can ride No-Name in the rally tomorrow."

"By dyeing my hair?" Lisa asked in confusion.

"No, no," Stevie said. "But remember, that dye I bought to use on you was dark brown, and it's the kind that washes out after a few shampoos. That's why I couldn't understand why you wouldn't let me try it."

Veronica spoke up. "I still don't get it," she said. "There's no way you'll be able to ride No-Name tomorrow.

Chelsea Webber and her sister are both in Pony Clubs—their whole family will probably be there."

"Veronica's right," Lisa said. "No matter what crazy scheme you have in mind, Stevie, there's no way it will work. Even if you dye your own hair and pretend to be someone else, Max still won't let you ride No-Name. You're stuck with Topside, any way you look at it."

"Looks can be deceiving, you know," Stevie said, patting Topside on the neck.

Carole was beginning to suspect she knew what Stevie had in mind. "Explain, Stevie," she said.

"Gladly," Stevie said. "Look at Topside, here. What color is he?"

Lisa shrugged. "He's a bay."

"Right. His coat is dark brown all over. Just about the same shade of dark brown that I wanted to dye your hair," Stevie said. "And just about the same shade as No-Name, except for her markings."

Lisa brushed back her light brown hair. "Are you saying what I think you're saying?" she asked incredulously. "You want to dye No-Name's hair?"

"You got it," Stevie confirmed. "If I dye her socks and stripe, she'll look like a solid bay, just like Topside. Nobody will recognize her."

"Chelsea will," Veronica reminded her. "Even as a solid bay, she'll at least suspect something's fishy, don't you think? After all, she'll probably be watching you closely."

Stevie shrugged. "Even if she does suspect, what can she do about it? It took a vet and an X-ray machine to prove No-Name's identity even *with* her markings. She'll never be able to prove a thing this way. And we'll get to beat Phil in the rally." And more important, Stevie added silently, she'd be able to ride *her* horse one more time before she had to give her up forever.

Carole and Lisa looked at each other. Then they looked at Stevie. Stevie looked back at them hopefully.

"Well, I think we should do it," Veronica declared before The Saddle Club could say a word. She smiled. "It'll be just the thing to get back at Chelsea Webber for taking your horse, Stevie." She patted Garnet. "I'll help you with the dye job. I should be good at it—I've watched the hairdresser dye my mother's hair often enough."

"Great!" Stevie said. She turned to Carole and Lisa. "Well?"

Carole hesitated. The plan was crazy—there was no doubt about it—but Stevie had managed to pull off equally outrageous stunts, with a lot less at stake. This time there was a horse involved—a beautiful part Arabian, part Saddlebred who belonged to Stevie, even if some stupid law said otherwise. And what could be more important than helping Stevie ride that horse one last time?

Carole took a deep breath, knowing quite clearly what she'd decided. "I'm in," she said quickly.

"Me, too," Lisa added. "But we've got to be careful. If

anyone finds out, you could be in big trouble, Stevie. We all could."

Stevie nodded. She didn't want to think too much about that—especially about what her parents would say if they found out. "I'll go home and get the dye right now. Can I borrow your bike, Lisa?" she asked.

Lisa nodded. "We'll get all the horses settled and meet you in No-Name's stall."

"Perfect," Stevie said. She handed Topside's reins to Carole. "I'll be right back."

Then she hurried off toward Lisa's bike, feeling better and more like herself than she had in days. Nothing cheered up Stevie more quickly than a sneaky and clever scheme.

THE FOLLOWING MORNING, Pine Hollow was abuzz with activity as Horse Wise members hurried to get ready to leave for the rally.

"All aboard for Cross County," Max called, striding down the stable aisle. "The bus leaves in exactly half an hour, so start loading."

The "bus" was actually a caravan of several horse trailers driven by Max, Red O'Malley, and parent volunteers. Each horse attending the rally had been assigned a place in one of the trailers. Mrs. Reg would bring up the rear of the caravan driving Pine Hollow's big old station wagon. Any riders whose parents weren't driving to the rally would ride with her.

Carole's father, Colonel Hanson, had volunteered to

drive The Saddle Club and Veronica to Cross County. In the meantime, Colonel Hanson was helping the riders get ready to leave.

Right now, Carole and Lisa were doing their best to keep the colonel away from Topside's stall.

"Hold on, girls," he said after he'd finished helping Lisa load her tack onto one of the trailers. "I'll be back in a second. I want to go check and see how Stevie's holding up." Carole had been keeping her father updated about Stevie's problems with the Webbers, and Colonel Hanson was just as concerned about Stevie as his daughter was.

Colonel Hanson hadn't known much about horses when he'd become a Horse Wise parent volunteer. His ignorance about even the simplest facts about horses and horse care had caused Carole a lot of embarrassment at first. But since then, Colonel Hanson had learned a lot. And Carole was pretty sure that even if her father suddenly forgot almost everything he'd learned, he would still be able to tell that the slightly blotchy-looking bay horse in Topside's stall was a mare and not a gelding.

Luckily he was distracted once again when May Grover begged him to help her untangle her pony's reins.

"Thank goodness," Carole exclaimed to Lisa as soon as Colonel Hanson had disappeared after the younger girl. "This could be harder than we thought."

Lisa nodded. "Come on, let's go see how Stevie's doing."

They found her in Topside's stall. "Hi, guys," she greeted them.

"Hi. How's it going?" Carole asked, peering over the stall door at the horse inside. "Max wants everybody to start loading up for the trip to Cross County."

Stevie nodded. "It doesn't really seem fair that Phil has the home field advantage, does it?" she grumbled. Then she grinned. "But even that's not going to help him today," she added confidently. "Now that No-Name's back in, we'll be unbeatable."

The others couldn't help agreeing. No-Name was obviously feeling frisky and ready to go, and Stevie's mood had improved one hundred percent since the day before. They really would be hard to beat—if no one noticed the results of their cosmetic work, that is.

"I hope Max doesn't find that straw in the trash bin," Lisa said worriedly. They'd had some trouble getting No-Name to hold still for her dye job the afternoon before, and as a result a lot of sticky brown dye had ended up on the straw on the stall floor. Lisa had done her best to stuff the colored straw down among the trash in the big bin behind the stable, but if Max or Red happened to look down into the bin they'd be able to see it.

"Don't worry," said Stevie breezily. "Even if he does notice it, he's much too busy to start worrying about some dyed straw right now."

"You're probably right," Carole said. "Still, I think he

might find time to start worrying if he notices that the horse in No-Name's stall isn't No-Name. I just checked, and Topside's already started chewing off his socks." The girls had used white shoe polish to give the gelding uneven socks and an exclamation point on his face.

Stevie shrugged. "You guys worry too much," she said. "Nobody will notice a thing. And even if they do, what can they do to me—threaten to take away my horse?"

Carole and Lisa smiled a little at Stevie's black humor, then they all got back to work. Topside had been assigned a spot on Red's van with several other horses, including Starlight. Garnet and Prancer were in a different van. Lisa, Carole, and Veronica quickly loaded their horses, then went to Topside's stall to help Stevie.

"Okay, let's go," Stevie said, opening the stall door and leading No-Name out. "Lisa, you're on distraction patrol. Make sure Max is too busy to notice No-Name."

Lisa nodded and hurried away. She found Max and started asking him about stirrup leathers. Soon she, Max, and Mrs. Reg were heading for the tack room.

"Okay, Veronica," Stevie said as they reached the stable door. "You're in charge of Red."

"Got it," Veronica said. She strolled over to the van, where Red was helping Adam Levine finish loading his tack. "Oh, Red," Veronica sang out in a loud, whiny voice. "Could you get Garnet's tack for me?"

Stevie and Carole giggled at the look on Red's face,

which said as plain as day that he'd known the old Veronica would return soon enough. He sighed and headed for the tack room.

"All clear," Carole said. She and Stevie started toward the van with No-Name in tow.

"Uh-oh," Stevie said a moment later. "Concerned father at five o'clock."

Carole looked and saw her father hurrying toward them. "I'm on it," she said. She veered off, intercepting Colonel Hanson when he was still too far away to get a good look at the horse Stevie was leading. "Hey, Dad, I'm glad you're here," she exclaimed. "You've got to help me. Amie lost her lucky hat, and she's hysterical—she won't ride without it. Will you help me find it?"

Stevie was close enough to hear, and she silently congratulated her friend on her quick thinking. Pine Hollow had dozens of hard hats, which were stored on hooks on the wall in the student dressing room. It would take ages to look through all of them. By the time Carole pretended to find the one she was looking for, No-Name would be safely loaded.

Luckily, everyone else at Pine Hollow was distracted enough getting ready themselves that none of them noticed the unfamiliar and rather blotchy bay mare that Stevie was loading on the van. When The Saddle Club and Veronica met up at the Hansons' station wagon a few minutes before departure, they traded winks.

"Operation Beauty Parlor is successful so far," Stevie whispered.

The others giggled, then climbed into the car.

BEFORE LONG THE Pine Hollow caravan arrived at Cross County and started unloading. Once again there was a whirlwind of activity, and Stevie saddled up No-Name without anyone's noticing her identity. Stevie tightened the mare's girth, then swung up into the saddle. It was time to ride her horse again—probably for the last time.

She distracted herself from that sad thought, by reminding herself that it was also time for Horse Wise to have their revenge against Phil's team. It was time to win!

The Pine Hollow riders lined up for inspection. Stevie crossed her fingers as Max went from horse to horse, making sure they were all ready to go. As he got closer, Stevie crossed her toes, too. There were some people who would be fooled by No-Name's disguise, but Stevie knew very well that Max wasn't one of them. She watched anxiously as he glanced over Starlight, who was next to No-Name.

Finally it was their turn. Max glanced at Stevie's mount, and his forehead furrowed as he gave the horse a puzzled frown. Then recognition dawned. "What are you thinking of?" he hissed at Stevie.

"I had to do it, Max," Stevie whispered back urgently. She had to make him understand. "This is my last chance to ride her. I just couldn't stand it if I missed it. I really couldn't." Stevie felt tears welling up behind her eyes, but she swallowed hard and held them back. No-Name reached out and nibbled at Max's collar.

"Don't you think people will find out?" he said quietly, stroking the mare's soft nose and gently detaching her lips from his collar.

"Not if you don't tell them," Stevie countered. She held her breath as she waited for Max's answer.

"Tell them what?" he said at last, and moved on down the row.

Stevie sighed with relief and glanced over at Carole. Carole gave her a questioning look, and Stevie gave her a smile and a thumbs-up sign. Her secret was safe with Max.

A few minutes later the rally began. Mr. Baker, the director of Cross County, explained how the competition would work. Eight different Pony Clubs were at the rally, and each club had two or three teams representing it, for a grand total of eighteen teams. Stevie, Carole, Lisa, and Veronica were one of the Pine Hollow teams; Adam Levine, Meg Durham, Simon Atherton, and Polly Giacomin were the other. Obviously, it would be difficult for that many teams to compete simultaneously. Therefore, there would be three elimination rounds. The top two teams in each round would make it to the final round to compete for ribbons.

"All right, everyone," Mr. Baker called, holding up a hard hat. "Your attention please. I'd like each team to send a representative up here to draw a piece of paper out of this hat. The number on the paper will determine which of the three rounds you're in."

"Go ahead, Stevie," Lisa said. "Pick us a number." Carole and Veronica nodded.

Stevie dismounted and handed No-Name's reins to Carole. Then she joined the group of eager riders gathered around Mr. Baker. Stevie picked out a slip of folded paper from the hard hat, then carried it back to her team without opening it. "Okay, guys," she said. "The moment of truth . . ." She opened the piece of paper. On it was a big number three.

"We're in the third group," Carole said. "That's good. It means we'll have an idea of what our competition is going to be in the final round."

Stevie grinned. "My thoughts exactly." She was glad that her friends seemed to be as eager to win as she was. If this was going to be her last day riding No-Name, she wanted it to be special.

The Saddle Club watched as the first group of teams—including Chelsea Webber's team from Mendenhall Stables, and the other Pine Hollow team—went through the first round of play. They started with an egg-and-spoon race. Chelsea's team was in last place until the final leg, when Chelsea and her horse, a tall, calm gray gelding, made up a lot of the lost ground and finished fourth. The Pine Hollow team came in last, thanks to Simon, who couldn't keep his egg on his spoon for more than three seconds.

In the races that followed, the first Pine Hollow team continued to do miserably. In the water race, Simon dropped the bucket three times. In the tabletop race, he lost his balance and slipped off the far side of Patch's saddle. In the ribbon relay, he got the long red ribbon he was carrying so tangled in his horse's mane that it took him several valuable seconds to work it loose so he could pass it to Polly.

The Saddle Club cheered loyally for their stablemates, but they couldn't help laughing at some of Simon's fumbles. At the same time, they couldn't help noticing how well Chelsea was doing, although her team ended up finishing fourth. Stevie was relieved—that meant there was no chance she'd have to compete against Chelsea in the finals.

Phil's team was in the second round, and finished first. Stevie cheered loudly for him the whole time. When her friends gave her questioning looks, she shrugged. "We can't beat the pants off him if he doesn't make it to the final round, right?" she said.

Her friends smiled. They had the funniest feeling that wasn't the only reason Stevie was cheering for her boyfriend. But they knew better than to say so.

Finally it was their turn. As Stevie rode No-Name into the ring, she cast a nervous glance in the direction of Chelsea Webber, who had returned her gelding to his stall and was sitting in the stands with her parents and sister. Stevie was more worried than she'd let on to her friends about the possibility that Chelsea would recognize No-Name, even with the disguise. But Chelsea didn't seem to suspect a thing so far.

The teams lined up for the egg-and-spoon race. Carole passed the spoon to Lisa without missing a beat. Veronica was next. As Stevie waited her turn, she glanced over at Chelsea again. The other team from Mendenhall Stables was competing in this round, and Chelsea was cheering enthusiastically for her stablemates. She didn't seem to be paying much attention to the Pine Hollow team at all, and Stevie was glad.

Then Veronica passed her the spoon, and Stevie forgot all about Chelsea, throwing herself into the fun of the game. No-Name was clearly having fun, too. After finishing first in the egg-and-spoon race, the Pine Hollow team went on to finish first or second in the other races as well, ending up in first place and advancing to the final round.

After a short break, the six top teams returned to the ring.

"Now the real competition starts," Stevie remarked to her teammates, glancing over at Phil.

"Uh-oh," Lisa and Carole said in one voice. But they were only kidding, and Stevie knew it. They all wanted to win. Having No-Name back on the team made it even more important for all of them.

One of the Cross County stable hands had set up a row of chairs in the center of the ring. "Great, musical chairs. We're awesome at that," Veronica remarked confidently. This was one of the few games where the riders had to perform individually rather than as teams. The four individual scores were added together to form the team score.

Veronica was proven correct a few minutes later, when Stevie finished in second place and Lisa finished fourth. Carole and Veronica were sixth and seventh.

Unfortunately, Phil came in first.

"We've got to do better in the next game," Stevie said grimly. No-Name tossed her head and stamped her foot.

The next race was an obstacle course relay race. This one took a few minutes to set up—it seemed that Mr. Baker had come up with the strangest things possible to use as obstacles, and he'd cooked up an incredibly intricate course among them. The winner was the team that made it through with the fewest mistakes or refusals. In the case of a tie the team with the faster time won.

Pine Hollow was the first team, and Stevie was riding the first leg. "Come on, girl, we can do it," she whispered to No-Name as they prepared to start. "Let's really show everyone that you and I are a team." No-Name's ears perked forward eagerly.

At the signal from Mr. Baker, Stevie urged her horse

forward. The first obstacle was a bucket of water. The horse had to pass between the bucket and the fence without knocking the bucket over.

"No drinks for you this time, okay?" Stevie told No-Name with a chuckle. She guided the mare between the fence and the bucket at a trot. No-Name glanced down at the bucket as she passed it, but obeyed Stevie and continued forward toward the next obstacle, a series of barrels. Under Stevie's careful guidance, the mare weaved her way among them without a misstep.

Next was a series of cavalletti, the long poles used in training horses to jump. That was an easy one. Stevie kept the mare at a trot, and No-Name adjusted her stride perfectly to avoid touching any of the cavalletti.

"Okay, we're almost halfway home," Stevie told her horse. "You're doing great."

The mare's ears flicked back for a second, listening, then she returned her full attention to the fence they were approaching. It was a low one, and No-Name cleared it easily. She responded instantly upon landing, when Stevie guided her sharply to the right and then brought her to a quick stop in front of a bale of hay.

Stevie dismounted. "Follow me," she urged the horse, leading her to the bale. No-Name followed and stepped up onto the bale without hesitation. A second later they were on the other side and Stevie was back in the saddle.

The next obstacle was the hardest for most riders. It was

a long, thick rope, which Mr. Baker had laid down in a snaky double-S-shaped pattern. The riders had to guide their horses along one side of the rope, as close as they could. But points were subtracted from their score if the horse stepped on or over the rope.

No-Name's hooves were so close to the rope that Lisa, Carole, and Veronica held their breath as they watched. It seemed impossible that the mare wouldn't miss a step somewhere along the way. But she didn't. Stevie and No-Name were working as a team, in perfect harmony.

After maneuvering over or around the few remaining obstacles, No-Name broke into a canter and raced to the finish line, where Lisa was waiting for her turn. Stevie was grinning uncontrollably. She knew they'd had a perfect round.

Stevie watched and cheered as the others made their way through the course. None of them did as well as Stevie and No-Name, but they didn't make many mistakes. They ended up coming in second to the team from Fairfax Stables. Phil's team came in third.

A few races later the three top teams—Pine Hollow, Cross County, and Fairfax—were neck and neck. The final two events, the four-abreast flag race and the costume race, would determine the order of finish.

In the four-abreast flag race, the four members of each team had to ride side by side, holding three separate flags between them. The flags were each about a yard long, and they weren't allowed to touch the ground during the race. That meant each team really had to perform as a team, keeping their paces and their spacing even. Since this took up a lot of space in the ring, the teams went one at a time. The team that finished fastest was the winner.

Cross County went first. "I hope you guys are ready for this," Phil said with a grin as he rode past The Saddle Club on his way to the ring. "We're about to set the time to beat."

He turned out to be right. The Cross County team worked in perfect harmony, their horses cantering side by side without a misstep or a dropped flag the whole way.

"Told you," he said, his grin bigger than ever, as he rode past Stevie again on his way out of the ring.

"Don't worry," Stevie assured him. "You've given us the time to beat, all right. And we're going to beat it."

But before Stevie could try to prove it to him, they had to wait for the other teams to go. The team from Linton Stables ended up dropping their flags twice and came nowhere near Cross County's time. The other two teams did better but were still several seconds behind. Then it was Fairfax's turn. Their final time was one second ahead of Cross County's.

"Wow," Carole said admiringly. "They were really good. That time's going to be hard to beat."

"Come on," Stevie replied. "Let's show them all how it's done."

The Saddle Club and Veronica entered the ring and lined up behind the starting line. Now they had to ride across the ring to the long table where the flags were laid out. They had to pick them up, turn the horses around, and head back across.

"On your marks," Mr. Baker said, "Get set . . . GO!"

The team took off. Seconds later all four horses screeched to a halt in front of the table. Stevie and No-Name were on one end, next to Veronica, so Stevie only had to grab the end of one flag. She waited for the others to pick up their ends, then signaled No-Name to turn, raising the hand holding the flag as they twisted around. The mare obeyed the command perfectly, as if horse and rider were one being, and Stevie's eyes wandered toward the stands where Chelsea was sitting. She wanted to make sure the other girl had seen how well Stevie and No-Name worked together—even if Chelsea didn't realize No-Name's true identity.

In that split second, Stevie's concentration wavered—and in that split second, the flag slipped out of her grasp.

"Oh, rats!" Stevie cried, grabbing futilely at the fluttering cloth. Veronica glanced over and saw what had happened. She tried to help, waving her end of the flag to try to move the other end within Stevie's grasp. But Stevie's hand just missed it at every try. Meanwhile Garnet had started forward. If Stevie didn't do something fast, this

105

would be a disastrous round for the team—it could mean the difference between winning and losing.

But before Stevie could do anything, No-Name stepped in. The mare looked around to see what was fluttering by her head. Spotting the waving flag, the mare grabbed it in her teeth and snorted. The cheering crowd burst out laughing.

Stevie's eyes widened. "Let's go!" she cried to her teammates.

Glancing over, the others saw what had happened. At Stevie's repeated urging, they surged forward, the four horses moving as one. No-Name kept the flag clenched tightly in her teeth. The horses cantered across the ring and over the finish line to loud cheers from the crowd. Even when the race was over, No-Name seemed reluctant to give up her end of the flag.

"I guess it must taste good," Lisa said as Stevie gently forced the mare's mouth open and dislodged the well-chewed piece of cloth.

"That's not why she did it," Stevie corrected, giving No-Name a hug and a kiss on the nose. "She was just helping out the team."

The others laughed. They really couldn't argue with that.

After scratching his head and checking his mental rule book, Mr. Baker declared that he saw no reason why a nonhuman member of the team couldn't carry the flag just as well as a human one. And after all, the flag hadn't touched the ground. The team ended up in third place.

"Not bad, considering the delay at the turn," Carole said.

"I know," Stevie agreed. "But we've got to win the last one. We've got to beat Phil."

No-Name's stunt had given the whole team a burst of additional energy. In the last event, the costume race, all four members threw the costumes on and off faster than ever before. Stevie and No-Name had the last leg, and they raced across the finish line a good six yards ahead of the rider from Fairfax, who came in second.

The judges conferred for a moment, then the results were official. The team from Fairfax was declared the day's champion. Stevie, Carole, Lisa, and Veronica had finished second, and Phil's team was third. Everyone cheered enthusiastically as the three teams lined up to receive their ribbons. Stevie shot Phil a triumphant look, and he gave her a mock salute and a sheepish grin in return.

As Stevie turned forward again, she noticed that even Chelsea was clapping and shouting for the winners. That made her feel a little strange, because it reminded her that this victory with No-Name, sweet as it was, would be her last. During the excitement of the last few races she had all but forgotten that.

"Congratulations, girls," said Ms. Cleese, the director of Linton Stables, who was one of the judges. She presented them with their red ribbons, clipping them onto each horse's bridle.

As she stepped away from No-Name, the judge glanced down at her hands, a slightly puzzled expression on her face. Lisa saw that Ms. Cleese's hands had dark brown smudges on them. The woman stared at her hands for a moment, then shrugged and wiped them off on her jeans. Lisa stifled a giggle and glanced over at Carole and Veronica, who were trying not to laugh as well.

Stevie hadn't even noticed what had happened, though. She was already getting ready to lead No-Name away, back to the van. The last thing she wanted was to give anyone, especially Chelsea Webber, the chance for a close-up look at No-Name.

As soon as the ribbon presentation was over Stevie headed back across the grounds to the Pine Hollow van. She untacked No-Name and led her into her compartment in the trailer. Then she spent a few minutes petting and talking to the horse.

"It was really great to ride you again," she told the mare softly. "Even if it was the very last time." In response, No-Name nibbled on Stevie's sleeve and snorted. "You don't even realize yet that they're going to take you away from me, do you?" Stevie whispered. She swallowed hard to hold back the unshed tears that were suddenly threatening to spill over once again. She wanted to enjoy this day as long as she could. There would be plenty of time to be sad later.

After a few more minutes, Stevie reluctantly left the horse alone and headed back toward the ring. She knew that Phil was scheduled to give a demonstration, and she didn't want to miss it.

As she walked back across the nearly empty grounds toward the crowded stands surrounding the ring, she heard voices from behind a nearby van. Stevie took a few more steps and then stopped in her tracks, staring in surprise. There, deep in serious conversation, were Veronica di-Angelo and Chelsea Webber.

Stevie furrowed her brow. What was going on? After the way Veronica had described her last conversation with Chelsea, Stevie couldn't believe the two girls would have anything polite to say to each other. But the discussion they were having now looked polite enough. Neither girl noticed Stevie watching them. A moment later Chelsea nodded, said something else, and then handed Veronica a piece of paper. Veronica patted her riding breeches but then seemed to realize they had no pockets. She dropped the paper into Garnet's grooming bucket, which was sitting on the ground at her feet. Then she picked up the bucket, nodded to Chelsea, and hurried away toward the Pine Hollow vans. Chelsea walked away in the opposite direction, toward the ring.

Stevie followed slowly, her mind a whirl. But at that moment Mr. Baker's voice came over the PA system, announcing that Phil Marsten was about to begin his demonstration. Stevie ran the rest of the way to the stands, sliding into the seat Carole was saving just as Phil entered the ring on his horse, Teddy.

"Check this out," Lisa said, leaning over to talk to Stevie. "Phil's going to demonstrate shooting a water pistol at a target while riding bareback."

"Didn't you teach him how to do that, Stevie?" Carole asked.

Stevie grinned, forgetting all about Veronica and Chelsea. "You bet I did." She watched as Phil rode over and shot—bulls-eye! "See what a good teacher I am?"

The rest of Phil's demonstration went just as well. Stevie enjoyed it, but she found her mind wandering frequently back to the spirited mare in the horse trailer nearby. It still didn't seem fair that she and Stevie would be separated soon. Stevie's mind kept going around in circles, trying to figure out a way to keep it from happening. But another part of her mind knew it was useless. She had ridden her horse for the last time.

As the demonstration ended and the crowd began to disperse, Max found Stevie. "Young lady, I'd like to speak to you for a moment," he said, pulling her aside.

Stevie glanced back at her friends and gulped. Just because Max had let her ride No-Name in the rally didn't mean he wasn't going to chew her out for the stunt she'd pulled. She just hadn't expected him to do it so soon.

"Max, I'm really sorry for trying to trick everyone like

that," she began. "It's just like I told you, though—I really wanted to ride her one more time, and—"

"Stevie," he interrupted, holding up one hand. "That's not what I was going to say. I think you know the risk you took by disobeying the restraining order. And I think you know better than to try anything like that again. You could have gotten yourself, your friends, and me into a lot of trouble."

Stevie nodded meekly. "I know. I'm sorry."

"What I wanted to say," Max said, with just the hint of a smile, "is that you'd better make sure to get that mare cleaned up as soon as we get back to Pine Hollow. And Topside, too, if you did something crazy like painting socks onto him."

Stevie's face turned red. She nodded.

Max broke into a full smile. "I see. Well, then, clean him up, too. If we're lucky, nobody else will ever have to know a thing about this. Now come on, let's get to work." He and Stevie headed toward the area where the Pine Hollow vans were parked. "By the way, Stevie," Max said as they walked. "You and No-Name were great together today. It's rare to see a horse and rider so perfectly matched."

Stevie turned to look at him. He looked back, his expression somber. Stevie realized that although he might not show it, Max knew what she was going through. "Thanks, Max," Stevie whispered.

*   *   *

LATER, AS THE GIRLS rode back to Pine Hollow in the Hansons' station wagon, Carole, Lisa, and Veronica chatted about everything that had happened that day. Stevie sat in the front seat, silently fingering her red ribbon and remembering the important role No-Name had played in their victory.

She looked ahead at the horse van trundling down the road in front of the car. It was nice to think that No-Name was in that van just ahead of them, and that when they arrived at the stable she'd be waiting for Stevie to take care of her. Even if Stevie had ridden her for the last time, No-Name was still hers for a little while longer.

Stevie tried to convince herself to be happy about that. But it was all she could do to keep from bursting into tears. No matter how wonderful the rally had been today, it was over now, and Stevie knew that in a few short days No-Name would be taken from her and she would never see her again. She promised herself she would stay away from No-Name because she couldn't bear the thought of watching Chelsea Webber on her mare. Instead she would face the future bravely, without her very special, very own, wonderful spirited perfect horse. She could almost see that future now, stretching ahead like the wide black road they were driving on, bleak and empty.

ON TUESDAY, STEVIE went straight home after school instead of heading over to Pine Hollow as usual. Today was the day the judge was supposed to decide officially whether No-Name and Punk were, indeed, one and the same horse.

She opened the kitchen door quietly and stepped inside. Both her parents were there waiting for her. The looks on their faces told Stevie everything she needed to know.

"We lost, didn't we?" Stevie said, her lip trembling.

"I'm so sorry, honey," her mother replied. "The judge considered all the evidence and declared that No-Name is the Webbers' horse. We've been ordered to return her this afternoon."

Stevie had been expecting this news for days and thought she was prepared for it. But hearing it was still like getting a pair of hooves in the stomach. There was nothing she could say or do. It was over. There was no hope of keeping No-Name any longer. Tears streamed freely down Stevie's face. Her parents let her cry. Then Mr. Lake spoke up softly.

"Max is letting us borrow one of his trailers. I can take her myself if you'd rather not be there."

Stevie shook her head. She was still unable to talk.

"No, I want to come with you," she said finally. "And I'd like to groom her before we go, if there's time."

Her father nodded. "Of course there is," he said gently. "The Webbers aren't expecting us for an hour or two anyway. Come on, I'll drive you over to Pine Hollow now."

A few minutes later Mr. Lake dropped Stevie off by the front gate of Pine Hollow. "I'll be back in an hour or so, okay?" he said.

Stevie nodded, then hurried inside. She went straight to No-Name's stall. As she started to slide open the door, Carole poked her head out over the partition of Starlight's stall next door, where she was preparing for class.

"Hi, Stevie," she said. "Any news?"

Stevie just nodded. She couldn't speak, because her eyes were filling up with tears once again and she didn't trust her voice. Luckily, Carole understood immediately.

"Oh, Stevie!" she whispered, her own dark eyes growing wet. She came out of the stall and gave her friend a hug. "Does Lisa know yet?"

114

Stevie shook her head and swallowed hard. "No," she said, her voice only shaking a little. "I just got here. My dad's coming back in an hour to help me take her over to the Webbers'."

"Are you sure you want to go along when he—well, when he takes her away?" Carole asked, concern in her voice.

"I'm sure," Stevie said. "I have to be there to say good-bye."

"Do you want me and Lisa to come with you?" Carole asked. "I'm sure Max would understand if we skipped class."

"No," Stevie said. "Thanks, but I have to say good-bye by myself."

Carole squeezed Stevie's hand. "I understand. That's what I would want to do if it were Starlight. You know where we are if you need us," she added. "I'll let Lisa know what's happening for you if you want."

"Thanks," Stevie said again. She let herself into No-Name's stall. The mare greeted her by snuffling at her hair. Stevie reached out and gave her a big hug.

She felt the mare's silky coat and breathed deeply to smell her pungent horsey scent. The warmth of the mare's body gave Stevie the strength to continue.

"Hi, girl," she whispered. "I hope you're ready for the grooming of your life, because that's what you're about to get."

Stevie started by rubbing off the last traces of the temporary hair dye from No-Name's head and legs. The Saddle Club had cleaned up both No-Name and Topside as soon as they'd arrived back at Pine Hollow on Saturday, but a few stubborn flecks of brown had remained on No-Name's white parts. Now Stevie made sure to remove every last one, using brush, rag, and fingernails. Soon the mare's markings were gleaming white again.

Then it was time for the serious grooming to begin. Stevie took special care picking out the mare's hooves, making sure there wasn't so much as a speck of dust in them. Then she painted all four hooves with hoof oil. She went over No-Name's deep brown coat with a dandy brush, then a body brush. Next she sponged off the mare's fine-boned head, taking extra care around the big dark eyes.

Throughout the grooming, No-Name snuffled and sighed, obviously taking great pleasure in being fussed over. Stevie talked softly to the mare, telling her over and over how much she'd loved their short but special time together. "After all," Stevie murmured as she finished combing out the mare's mane and tail and started to go over her body once more with a soft brush. "As horrible as it is to lose you, it's still better than if I never knew you at all." The mare snorted and half-closed her eyes, enjoying the feel of the brush on her back.

By the time Mr. Lake returned, Stevie was sure No-Name looked as beautiful as she'd ever looked in her life.

While her father and Red O'Malley went to bring out the horse van, Stevie spent a few final moments alone with her horse, feeding her some sweet baby carrots she'd bought the day before and talking to her quietly. Stevie was determined to face this ordeal one minute at a time. She wouldn't think about what was coming. She'd just try to savor these last few precious minutes with No-Name.

Then it was time to load the mare onto the van. No-Name docilely followed Stevie up the ramp and stood quietly while Stevie tied her in place. Stevie helped her father close the door, and they climbed into the cab of the van. Stevie knew better than to ask to ride in the back with the horse—that could be dangerous to both of them. Instead, she spent the fifteen-minute ride to the Webbers' house with her nose pressed to the glass window separating the cab from the back. She didn't say a word the whole way. She was too busy just staring at her beautiful horse. Her father talked to her for the first few miles, telling her some of the legal details. He explained that he would be able to recover the money he'd paid Mr. Baker for No-Name, Mr. Baker could recover the money from the person he'd bought her from, and so on down the line. There was a slight chance somebody might find the person who had stolen her from the Webbers. When Stevie still didn't say a word, Mr. Lake fell silent as well, concentrating on his driving for the rest of the trip.

Stevie's stomach contracted as her father slowed down

and turned into a long gravel driveway. He drove slowly over the bumpy surface past a large white farmhouse, until they reached the small barn behind the house. Then he stopped the van and turned to Stevie.

"Well, kid, this is it," he said softly. "Are you ready?"

She gulped and blinked back the tears that threatened to brim over onto her cheeks. She promised herself she wouldn't show the Webbers how much she hurt. "As ready as I'll ever be," Stevie told her father. She turned and hopped out of the cab. Then she hurried around to the back of the van and started to swing open the door, just as the back door to the house opened and Chelsea hurried out. Her parents and sister were right behind her.

Stevie's father went to greet them as Stevie entered the van and unhooked No-Name's lead rope.

"Come on, girl," Stevie said. "Let's go. There are some people waiting for you outside."

She carefully led the mare out of the van. The Webbers watched silently. Then Chelsea stepped forward and gave No-Name a big hug. "Thanks for bringing Punk home, Stevie," she said, sounding a little tentative. "Do you want to help me put her in her stall?"

Stevie nodded, surprising herself. She hadn't expected to want to help Chelsea get No-Name settled, but somehow it felt right. She and No-Name followed Chelsea into the small barn, which contained a few large, comfortable stalls.

118

Stevie noticed the tall gray gelding Chelsea had ridden in the rally peering over the top of one of them.

Chelsea followed her gaze. "That's the horse my parents rented for me when Punk was stolen. His name is Silverado." She stopped in front of an empty box stall. "This one's Punk's. I've got it all clean and ready for her."

Stevie nodded again. She turned to No-Name and gave her a quick hug. Then she stared down at the lead rope clenched in her hand. She didn't want to give it up. Instead, she wanted to turn and lead her horse out of this strange barn, back to Pine Hollow where she belonged. Forever. For a split second she almost started to do just that. But then she bit her lip and handed the lead rope to Chelsea. "Here, you can take her in."

Chelsea accepted the lead and led the horse into the stall. Stevie could hear her talking softly to the mare, who nickered a few times as if in response to her words.

Stevie didn't even try to hear what Chelsea was saying. She just watched No-Name, memorizing the lines of her head, the look in her eyes, and the way she moved. She let her eyes run down the smooth arch of her mare's neck, past the stubborn little strand of mane that always flopped over onto the wrong side. And then Stevie's gaze turned to the markings on No-Name's face, as unique as the horse herself. The mare reached down and nibbled at Chelsea's blond hair.

Then Stevie turned away, suddenly unable to watch

anymore. She knew she'd never meet another horse like No-Name, not ever. In a flash of understanding, she realized that that was why Chelsea was so happy to have her back. But understanding it didn't make it any easier to bear. Stevie had never wanted anything as much as she wanted this horse. She couldn't imagine how she would manage to go on without her, to wake up every day knowing that her beloved horse belonged to somebody else and that Stevie might never so much as see her again. She felt like screaming out with all the anger and sadness and frustration she felt at this moment, but she knew it wouldn't do any good. There was nothing she could do to stop her heart from breaking.

A moment later Chelsea let herself out of the stall. No-Name stretched her head out over the half door for one last nibble at her hair. Chelsea laughed and pushed the horse's head away. "That's her worst habit," she said. She glanced at Stevie. "But I guess you probably knew that already," she added more quietly. Stevie could tell the other girl felt sorry for her. She realized that Chelsea wasn't a bad person at all. She obviously loved No-Name a lot. But that didn't make Stevie feel any better. She knew that no matter how much Chelsea loved the mare, Stevie loved her just as much—or more. Nothing would change that.

"Would you like to say good-bye to her?" Chelsea asked. "I could wait outside."

"Thanks," Stevie said. She waited until Chelsea left, then let herself into the box stall. "This looks like a nice place to live," she said to the horse. Then she started scratching all No-Name's special itchy places while she talked. "You be good for Chelsea, okay? She loves you and she'll take good care of you. And maybe we'll see each other at Pony Club rallies and shows, right? It won't be the same as being together all the time, but . . ."

Stevie's voice trailed off as the tears she'd been holding back all afternoon came at last. This was really it. She was losing her horse—forever. She would never ride her again, never groom her again, never feed her special treats or bed her down for the night. She wouldn't get to feel No-Name's soft lips nibbling her hair when the mare was in a particularly playful mood, or try to outthink her when No-Name was being stubborn. She wouldn't even know if the mare was happy, or healthy, asleep, or awake. There would be a million little moments that she would never be able to share with her. There would be a lifetime of good times and companionship she would be missing. And she knew she would miss every second of it. Stevie sobbed inconsolably, burying her face in No-Name's silky coat, while the mare stood quietly.

But finally No-Name lowered her head and nibbled at Stevie's hair. Stevie laughed through her tears and stepped back to look at the horse. "You're one of a kind, No-Name, you know that?" she said. She wiped her face on the sleeve of her shirt. "I'd better go now, girl. Good-bye." She gave her one last quick hug, then let herself out of the stall, willing herself not to start crying again.

She glanced back when she reached the barn door. No-Name was staring after her, her head stretched over the stall door. She nickered once.

"Good-bye," Stevie whispered. For a second that felt like an eternity, she gazed at the horse, making sure the picture of her standing there, her proud head held high, was stamped on her heart so clearly that it could never fade. She knew she would never forget one single second of the time they'd spent together—not if she rode a million other horses. Not ever.

Then Stevie turned away and went outside.

The others were waiting for her. "Come on, honey," her father said. "Let's go home." He shook hands with Mr. and Mrs. Webber and Chelsea, then led Stevie back to the van.

She climbed inside and slumped into the corner of the seat, staring out the window at the rolling Virginia landscape all the way home. But she didn't see a bit of it. All she could see, as tears streamed down her face, was the picture of her horse watching alertly as Stevie left her behind forever.

AFTER SCHOOL TWO days later, Stevie was still moping around the house. She lay facedown on her bed, thinking about No-Name. Stevie hadn't been to Pine Hollow since the mare had gone back to the Webbers'. She missed No-Name more and more every day. She still could hardly believe that the horse wasn't hers anymore, and never would be again. She kept reminding herself that Chelsea must have been just as miserable when No-Name was stolen as Stevie herself was now, but that only made her feel worse. It didn't seem fair that either one of them had to be miserable. But there didn't seem to be any way around it.

The phone rang, and her mother called up to her. "Stevie! It's Lisa!"

Stevie dragged herself into a sitting position and reached for the phone extension on her bedside table. She talked to Lisa for a few minutes, but her heart wasn't really in the conversation. Lisa told her all about what had happened at Pine Hollow that day, but Stevie couldn't seem to find it in herself to care about Prancer's antics or the new litter of stable kittens. Finally she excused herself, saying she had homework to do.

A few minutes later Carole called. Stevie suspected she must have been talking to Lisa, because she seemed even more determined than Lisa had been to cheer up Stevie. She told a funny story about Simon Atherton tripping over the bridle he was carrying and falling into the grain bin. Ordinarily this would have had Stevie in stitches. But today she couldn't even crack a smile.

Finally Carole seemed to realize it was hopeless. "Stevie," she said seriously. "I know you're still sad about No-Name, and you probably will be for a long time, but you can't let it ruin your life."

Stevie just sighed into the phone in response.

"Promise me you'll come to Pine Hollow on Saturday," Carole said.

"I don't know. . . ." Stevie began.

"Come on," Carole urged. "Topside misses you. Max has been letting Meg ride him, and the poor horse is tired of listening to her giggle through the whole lesson."

Stevie *almost* smiled at that. She could practically picture dignified Topside rolling his big brown eyes at Meg Durham's high-pitched laughter. "Well, maybe," she said.

"Promise me," Carole said firmly.

"All right, all right," Stevie gave in reluctantly. "I'll be there."

She said good-bye and hung up, then flopped back down on her bed. Her cat, Madonna, wandered in and saw her there. She jumped up onto the bed, lay down next to Stevie, and started to purr. Stevie stroked the cat's fur absently and went back to thinking about No-Name.

A few minutes later her father knocked on the door and came in. "Hi, sweetheart," he said. "How are you holding up?"

"Not so well," Stevie replied honestly. "I just miss her so much."

Mr. Lake nodded. "I'm sorry, honey," he said sympathetically. "I just came to tell you that the paperwork is complete. Your mother and I got our money back from Mr. Baker—and even better, the police think they know who stole Punk from the Webbers in the first place."

Stevie just shrugged. She didn't really care who had stolen No-Name. The only thing she cared about was that she didn't own her anymore.

"You know, Stevie, your mother and I were talking," Mr. Lake continued. "We intend to buy you another horse as soon as you're ready. Only this time we're going to find one with a clear line of ownership right back to the day of its birth!"

Stevie sighed. "Thanks, Dad," she said. "But I'm not sure I'll be ready for that anytime soon. It's not like replacing a broken toy or a worn-out pair of shoes or something. It won't be easy to find a horse to replace her."

"I understand," her father said. "No-Name was a special horse. We all know that. But moping around the house like you have been isn't going to do anybody any good—least of all you. It might be better to start looking at other horses right away. Maybe that will take your mind off No-Name a little."

Stevie shrugged again. "I doubt it."

"Come on," her father said. "When you fall off a horse, aren't you supposed to get right back on again? This is sort of the same thing, right?"

"Not really," Stevie said. "Thanks again, Dad. But I think I'll just stick to riding Topside for a while."

Her father nodded. "Well, if that's the way you want it."

"It is," Stevie replied. But as her father left the room, she thought to herself that it really wasn't what she wanted at all. What she wanted was to have No-Name back again. And that wasn't ever going to happen.

13

"IS STEVIE HERE YET?" Carole asked Lisa on Saturday morning.

"I haven't seen her," Lisa replied. "She did promise she'd come, didn't she?"

Carole nodded. "I called her again last night to make sure. She said she'd be here."

Suddenly Lisa nudged her. "Here she comes," she whispered. The two girls turned and watched as Stevie came down the stable aisle toward them.

"Hi, Stevie," Carole and Lisa said in one voice.

"Hi," Stevie replied glumly.

Carole searched her mind desperately for something cheery to say to her friend. She was saved by the arrival of

127

Meg Durham and Betsy Cavanaugh, who were coming from the tack room.

"Hi, Stevie," Betsy said, hoisting her saddle onto her other arm. "We heard about your horse. I'm really sorry."

"Me, too," Meg added. Both girls stared at Stevie with sympathy in their eyes.

"Thanks," Stevie said. "I appreciate it."

"Well, we better get going," Betsy said after a moment of silence. "We only have a few minutes before the Horse Wise meeting starts."

The two girls hurried away.

"Come on, Stevie," Lisa said. "We'd better get tacked up." The meeting that week was an unmounted one, but the guest speaker was the manager of the local tack shop. He wanted the riders to have their horses tacked up so he could show each of them how to check over every piece of metal and leather on his or her horse.

Stevie nodded and trailed along behind her friends as they headed for the tack room. When they arrived, Polly Giacomin was there.

"Oh, hi, you guys," she said when she saw them. "Stevie, I've been meaning to tell you how sorry I am that you lost No-Name." She grabbed her horse's bridle from its hook. "I don't know what I'd do if someone tried to take Romeo away from me." Romeo was Polly's horse, a spirited brown gelding.

"Well, I hope you never have to find out," Stevie told her. "It's not fun, I can tell you that."

Polly nodded sympathetically. "Well, try to hang in there, Stevie." She picked up Romeo's saddle and left.

"What else can I do?" Stevie muttered.

Carole and Lisa exchanged glances. They had hoped that coming to Pine Hollow would help Stevie's mood, at least a little. But apparently it hadn't.

The door opened again and Veronica strolled in. "Oh, there you are, Stevie," she said. "I've been looking for you. I wanted to give you my condolences about No-Name. The whole thing really stinks."

"Tell me about it," Stevie said forcefully.

"It's all that Chelsea Webber's fault," Veronica went on, bending over to rub a spot off her shiny brown boots. "She's so selfish it's incredible."

"Are those new boots, Veronica?" Lisa asked quickly. The last thing she wanted was to see Veronica set Stevie off on a conversation about Chelsea.

Veronica stood up quickly. "Yes," she said. "My mother took me to the mall last night and bought them for me."

"They're really nice," Lisa said, taking a closer look. "They must have been expensive." The minute the words left her mouth she remembered the diAngelo's financial situation and bit her lip.

But Veronica just said, "They were," and then changed

129

the subject. "Stevie, could I talk to you privately for a minute?" she asked.

Stevie shrugged. "Sure." She followed Veronica out of the tack room.

Veronica led her over to the stall that had been No-Name's. "Listen, Stevie," she began haltingly, looking down at her hands. "Things aren't going so well for my dad —you know, at work."

"He hasn't found those papers yet?" Stevie asked, once again feeling a little ashamed of herself for getting so caught up in her own problems that she forgot about other people's.

Veronica shook her head. "It's looking more and more like I might have to sell Garnet," she said, her voice breaking on the last two words. She took a deep breath. "And, well, I was just wondering whether—whether you would be interested in buying her."

Stevie was taken aback. "Me? Buy Garnet from you?"

Veronica nodded. "That way you'll have a wonderful new horse to replace No-Name, and I'll still be able to see Garnet—maybe even ride her once in a while if you'll let me. It makes perfect sense, don't you think?"

"Well . . ." Stevie paused to think about it. The thought had never crossed her mind, but now that it had, it *did* make a surprising amount of sense.

Stevie closed her eyes and tried to picture it. Garnet was a beautiful, sweet-tempered, purebred Arabian. She had a lot of potential as a show horse, though most of that potential had gone to waste so far, since Veronica wasn't interested in the hard work of training her. But Stevie knew that if *she* owned Garnet, she could train her to be a champion. She could almost picture herself in the saddle of the sturdy, wonderful mare, accepting blue ribbon after blue ribbon. It was certainly a tempting thought.

Stevie opened her eyes. "I wish I could, Veronica," she said. "But I don't know—Garnet is pretty valuable. My parents are planning to get me another horse, but I don't think they were planning to spend as much as your parents will ask for her. I don't think they can afford it."

Veronica smiled. "You know, Stevie, it's amazing the way parents can come up with extra money when they have to," she said. "They're probably feeling pretty guilty right now about this whole No-Name fiasco. I bet they'd be willing to spend a little more to make sure they know exactly what they're getting this time—especially if you convince them that Garnet is the only horse that can replace No-Name."

Stevie shrugged. The argument was vintage Veronica, but it did make some sense. Maybe her parents *could* manage the extra money—especially if they could strike a deal with the diAngelos.

"I'll think about it," she told Veronica at last.

Veronica nodded. "You really should," she said.

*   *   *

131

AFTER THE HORSE Wise meeting, the students had a few free minutes before they started their flat class. Stevie loosened Topside's girth and stowed him in his stall. Then she went to find her friends.

"Hey, can you guys come here for a minute?" Stevie asked Carole and Lisa when she found them at Prancer's stall. "I want to talk to you about something." She'd been thinking about Veronica's offer all through the meeting, and she'd reached a decision.

"What is it?" Lisa asked.

"Just come on," Stevie urged, heading toward the feed room.

Once all three girls were inside, settled comfortably on some sweet-smelling bags of grain, Stevie told them about her conversation with Veronica.

"It was a tempting thought," she finished. "I mean, Garnet is a great horse. . . ."

"And she does deserve a better rider than Veronica," Carole interrupted.

"Agreed," Stevie said. "But I don't think I'm that rider." She shrugged. "I may be capable of tricking my parents into a lot of things, but spending five times more than they can afford on a horse isn't one of them. Purebred or no purebred."

"It figures that Veronica would try to convince you to go along with her plan," Carole remarked.

"That's true," Lisa agreed. "Having an expensive pure-

132

bred horse is so important to her she probably thought that alone would be enough to convince you."

"It's not," Stevie said. "Garnet is beautiful, that's for sure. But No-Name showed me that a horse's breeding isn't the most important thing. It's what's in her heart that's even more important."

"True," Carole said. "If only Veronica could figure that out, she might actually turn into a normal person all the time instead of just once in a while."

"Oh, I don't know," Stevie said thoughtfully. "I never thought I'd say this, but I think she really does care about Garnet for her own sake. Otherwise she never would have come up with this plan to convince me to buy her."

"That's true," said Lisa logically. "After all, if she cared about Garnet only because of how valuable she was, she'd probably rather sell her to a stranger than to someone she knows."

"Right," Stevie said.

"I don't know," Carole said skeptically. "I'm still not sure I really trust her yet. A leopard can't totally change its spots."

"That's what I always thought, but I'm not so sure now," Stevie said. "Veronica has really been sympathetic about No-Name—just like a real friend." She thought back to the way Veronica had stuck up for her when Chelsea had showed up at Pine Hollow.

That reminded her of another time she'd seen the two

girls together—at the second Pony Club rally. "Wait a minute," she said, frowning slightly. "I might have to take that back." She described the conversation she'd witnessed, when Chelsea had handed Veronica a piece of paper.

"I wonder what that was all about?" Lisa said. "What could they possibly have to talk about after what Veronica told us she said to her?"

"I have no idea," Carole said. "But I know one thing. If Veronica put a piece of paper in Garnet's grooming bucket, I'll bet you an ice-cream sundae it's still there."

"No bet. I'm sure you're right," Stevie said. "Veronica probably never even put away the bucket after the rally. If it's not still in the van, it's probably sitting in Garnet's stall waiting to be kicked over or stepped in."

The girls hurried to the stall to look. The mare greeted them affectionately, and they paused for a second to pat her. Then they peered over the stall door. The bucket wasn't inside. "So much for that plan," Stevie said.

"Look!" Carole cried from behind her. "That must be it." She pointed to a bucket that someone had hung from a hook in the aisle. "Red or someone must have found it in the stall and hung it there out of harm's way."

"I can't believe it's been there for a whole week and Veronica hasn't even noticed," Lisa said in disgust. "She must have walked right past it a dozen times since last Saturday."

Stevie grabbed the bucket and peered inside. "Believe it or not, it's true," she cried triumphantly. She pulled a folded piece of paper out of the jumbled mess of combs and rags inside the bucket. "Voila! Here's the answer to the mystery."

Carole and Lisa peered over her shoulder as she unfolded the paper and read it.

"It looks like a reward notice," Lisa said.

Carole gasped. "Oh! The Webbers must have posted these when No-Name was stolen from them." She pointed. "See? There's their names and phone number, and a description of the horse."

"And a notice about the thousand-dollar reward," Stevie finished grimly. "You know what this means, don't you?"

"Not really," Carole admitted. "I mean, what does the reward have to do with Veronica?"

"Everything," Stevie said. She angrily crumpled the paper into a ball and clenched it in her hand. "Veronica sold me out. It all makes sense now."

"But Veronica wasn't the one who told the Webbers you had their horse," Carole argued. "Chelsea spotted her at the rally."

"But the Webbers needed solid proof before they could claim her," Lisa said slowly, catching on.

Stevie nodded. "Exactly," she said. "Veronica had to be the one who told the Webbers about No-Name's allergy to weeds. That was what clinched the identification—the

135

X-ray just confirmed it." Her eyes widened. "Come to think of it, she probably told them about the bone splint, too. That's why the Webbers were certain enough about No-Name's identity to send the letter with the restraining order so quickly."

"But the Webbers probably would have managed to prove No-Name and Punk were the same horse even without Veronica's help," Lisa said. "I mean, they already knew that Punk had the weed allergy and the bone splint. I'm sure they would have checked for those things eventually anyway."

"True," Carole admitted. "But her information certainly didn't hurt. And besides, that's not really the point."

"Right," Stevie growled. "The point is, Veronica is such a low, greedy, money-grubbing jerk that she stabbed me in the back just for the sake of that reward."

"Wow," Carole said softly. "I didn't think even Veronica could be that greedy. She sold you down the river for a thousand dollars. I guess she really wanted those expensive boots. Or maybe she needed to pay her hairdresser's bill for those highlights."

"It wasn't just the money," Lisa pointed out. "I bet she did it for Garnet, too. She knew if Stevie didn't have a horse, she'd have a better chance of talking her into buying Garnet."

Stevie was seething. "What a worm! What a low-down, bottom of the bucket, rotten awful thing to do," she exclaimed. "Veronica hasn't changed for the better—she's changed for the worse! Now she hides her rottenness under a nice exterior. I can't believe I was starting to think I could actually be friends with her."

"She can't get away with this," Carole said. "We've got to get back at her."

"And how," Stevie said grimly. "I think we should start with bamboo slivers under her fingernails, then maybe . . ."

Whatever Stevie had in mind next was drowned out as the PA system crackled to life. It was Mrs. Reg, saying there was a phone call for Stevie Lake in her office.

"I wonder who that could be?" Carole said.

Stevie shrugged. "I'll find out," she said. She left her friends and hurried to Mrs. Reg's office off the tack room. Mrs. Reg wasn't there, but she'd left the receiver lying on her desk.

Stevie picked it up. "Hello?"

"Hello, Stevie?" said the voice on the other end of the line. "This is Chelsea Webber. . . ."

14

"THAT'S THEIR DRIVEWAY," Stevie said, pointing ahead.

"Okay," replied Deborah Hale, Max's fiancée. She turned the wheel of Max's station wagon and the big car trundled over the bumpy gravel of the Webbers' driveway. "So you really don't have any idea what this is about?"

Stevie shook her head. "All Chelsea said was that I should come over right away." Stevie's mind had been racing since she'd hung up the phone a short while ago. The call from Chelsea had been so unexpected, and the message so mysterious, that Stevie was nearly sick with worry. Was something wrong with No-Name? Was that why Chelsea wanted Stevie to come over—so she could blame her for it? Maybe the hair dye had made the mare sick. Or maybe she had eaten something she shouldn't have.

138

Stevie's head whirled with one terrifying possibility after another.

"Here we are," Deborah said, bringing the car to a stop beside the house.

"Thanks, Deborah," Stevie said. "I'm glad you were around to drive me over here. I think I would have died if I'd had to wait for my parents to get home." After Stevie had hung up the phone, she had searched frantically for Max or Mrs. Reg. But Max was already in the ring beginning the flat class, and Mrs. Reg was nowhere to be found. Luckily, Deborah had turned up at just the right moment.

Stevie and Deborah got out of the car. As they did, Stevie noticed a flash of motion at one of the windows in the house. A moment later Chelsea appeared at the door. Her mother was with her.

"Hi, Stevie," Chelsea said as she approached. Stevie noticed that the other girl's eyes were red, as if she'd been crying. Stevie gulped. Whatever was wrong with No-Name, it must be something serious.

"Hi," Stevie replied tentatively. She introduced Deborah to the Webbers, then took a deep breath. "Why did you call me over here?" she asked, getting right to the point.

Mrs. Webber stepped forward. "Deborah, why don't you come inside for a cup of tea?" she offered. "I think the girls have some talking to do."

Deborah looked a little perplexed, but she nodded politely. "That would be lovely." She glanced at Stevie. "Will you be okay?"

Stevie nodded, feeling more confused than ever. What on earth was going on? How could Mrs. Webber talk about having tea when No-Name was sick?

The two adults headed into the house, and Chelsea started walking toward the barn. "Come on," she said shortly.

Stevie followed. "What is it, Chelsea?" she asked. "Just tell me. Is something wrong with No-N—I mean, with Punk?"

"No, nothing's wrong with her," Chelsea replied. She stopped just outside the barn door and turned to face Stevie. "It's just that I've made a terrible mistake."

Stevie frowned. "What are you talking about?" she asked. After all the emotional turmoil she'd been through in the past two weeks, the last thing she felt like doing right now was dealing with Chelsea Webber's problems. "Would you just tell me why I'm here?"

"I'm trying," Chelsea said. She took a deep breath. "You're here because—because I've realized that Punk is your horse, not mine. I mean, she *should* be yours. I want her to be yours."

"What?" Stevie was stunned. Was Chelsea saying what Stevie thought she was saying?

Chelsea swung open the barn door. "Come on inside. She's waiting for you."

Stevie followed her, still in a daze. But she snapped out of it when she heard a familiar whinny of greeting. "No-Name!" she cried, rushing forward to greet the mare.

Chelsea watched the reunion from a short distance away. "I think I made the right choice now," she said, more to herself than to Stevie.

Stevie turned. "But what—I mean, why—I mean—" she said, the words tumbling over one another. She stopped herself, then tried again. "Are you saying what I think you're saying?" she asked. "Are you saying I can have No-Name back?"

Chelsea nodded. "I think it's the best thing," she said. "My parents will sell her to you for the same price you paid before. You can take her whenever you're ready."

In a rush, all the sadness and bleakness that had hung over Stevie for the past week lifted, leaving her feeling happier than she could ever remember feeling. She opened the stall door and rushed inside to give No-Name a giant hug. The mare nickered softly in return. "Oh, No-Name! Can it be true? You're going to be mine again!" Stevie cried, her face pressed against the horse's coat, not caring what Chelsea thought.

After a moment, she tore herself away. She had to know how this miracle had happened. She left the stall, closed the door carefully, then turned to face Chelsea again. "What made you change your mind?" she asked.

141

Chelsea sat down on a bale of hay. "It's kind of hard to explain," she began.

Stevie sat down beside her and listened. Both girls watched No-Name as Chelsea spoke.

"I think it started when I saw what you'd done to be able to ride her in the rally last Saturday," Chelsea said.

Stevie gasped. "You knew?"

Chelsea chuckled. "The second I laid eyes on her. But you did a good job on her disguise," she hastened to add. "I don't think most people would have noticed a thing."

"I should have known you'd recognize her," Stevie said. "But I was just so determined to ride her one more time."

"I know," Chelsea said. "That's what I realized when I saw her there. And I realized that you and Punk make a pretty good pair. Anyone who would come up with an idea like that must be almost as crazy and unpredictable as Punk is." She laughed. "I named her that because of her markings, you know, but the name really suits her personality, too. She's one wild and crazy girl."

"I know," Stevie said, smiling. "I guess I am, too, kind of. Although I'm sure that just about anyone else would call me an idiot for trying to pull a stunt like No-Name's disguise."

"Well, you got away with it, didn't you?" Chelsea reminded her. "I mean, nobody recognized her except me. And the whole thing made me realize something. If you'd risk everything just to have one last chance to ride Punk, I

142

knew you must really love her. And I guess I hadn't really thought about that before. All I'd thought about was getting her back."

"Because you love her, too," Stevie said quietly.

Chelsea nodded. "I sure do," she said, staring at No-Name. "But I've realized since I got her back that she may not be the best horse for me. And I may not be the best rider for her. I've really never been able to ride her that well. She's thrown me or taken me by surprise more times than I can count."

"I can believe that," Stevie said. "She's quick."

"Right," Chelsea agreed. "Too quick for me, I think." She stood up and walked over to another stall. For the first time, Stevie noticed that the gray gelding, Silverado, was still inside it.

"Oh," Stevie said. "You haven't given him back yet?"

Chelsea shook her head and rubbed the gelding's nose fondly. "No, and I'm not going to," she said. "My parents are buying him for me. You see, when my parents first rented him, I was so upset about Punk's being stolen that I just sort of took him for granted. But when it was time to send him back I finally realized that he's actually a much better horse for me to ride than Punk ever was. Silverado and I are a great match. I didn't want to give him up. And then I realized how you must have felt having to give up Punk. After that, all I could think about was how sad you looked when you brought her here."

Chelsea looked down at her hands, and Stevie thought she saw tears in her eyes. "It took me a few days to really make up my mind to give Punk back to you. She and I have been together a long time, and we've learned a lot from each other. But you and Punk belong together, just like Silverado and I do. It's the best thing for all of us."

Stevie nodded. "I'm really glad you decided that," she said. She was impressed by the other girl's thoughtfulness. She realized she really hadn't given Chelsea enough credit —not only was she nicer than Stevie had thought, she was smarter and more mature, too. "And you can come visit her anytime you want."

"Thanks," Chelsea said. "Maybe I'll do that. And I'll see you guys at Pony Club rallies and stuff." She stood up and walked over to the mare's stall. Stevie followed. Chelsea opened the door and gave the mare a big hug. "I'll miss you, Punk. But Stevie will take good care of you."

When Chelsea stepped back, Stevie couldn't resist giving the horse a hug herself. She knew that Chelsea was feeling a little sad about giving up her horse, and she was sorry about that. But she knew that this was the way things should be. It felt so right to her that she knew Chelsea must feel it, too. Her heart brimming over with joy, Stevie stretched her arms as far around her horse as she could, hugging her so tightly that her horse let out a squeal of surprise and nosed Stevie's hair.

When she turned away from the mare, Stevie saw that

Chelsea was smiling. Stevie smiled, too. Then the two girls went to find Mrs. Webber and Deborah.

"Race you to the woods!" Stevie cried joyously. She signaled to her mare and the horse responded instantly, breaking into a gallop, galloping as fast as she could. She had a sleek elegance in her bloodlines—the speed and endurance of an Arabian, and the sassy beauty of the Saddlebred in her. It made a breathtaking combination and that thought made Stevie once again ponder the issue of her horse's name.

Punk wasn't right. Even if it was a cute name, based on the funny marking on the mare's face, it implied all sorts of things that just weren't true of this horse. No-Name wasn't worthy of her, either. She deserved a name that better reflected her own qualities. She was beautiful, strong, and brave. She had a way of fooling a rider into thinking she was meek, but that merely masked a stubborn streak that combined with her cocky confidence to remind Stevie of some of the belles of the American south, like Scarlett O'Hara. But Scarlett didn't suit her any better than Punk did.

Stevie's horse raced like the wind. Carole and Lisa raced to catch up, but the mare was too quick for them. She darted into the woods, where Stevie reluctantly pulled her back to a walk. But even at that slower pace, the mare pranced along briskly, looking curiously at the trees along

145

the sides of the path. She seemed to love the outdoors and the land—the trees and the grasses, though not the weeds!—and was totally content to be with Stevie in the woods. Moments later, they reached the shady spot by the creek.

Stevie dismounted and clipped a lead line onto her mare's halter. "Time to take a break," she said, giving her a hug. Just then Carole and Lisa arrived. "No fair," Carole called. "You had a head start."

Stevie grinned. "It doesn't matter," she said. "We should have won anyway. This horse wanted to win."

Carole and Lisa dismounted and secured their horses as well. Then the three girls went over to the creek and settled on one of the big rocks on its banks where they could watch the cold water rushing by.

"This is nice," Lisa said with a contented sigh. "Even if it is still too cold to put our feet in."

Stevie nodded, then looked over at her horse. The mare leaned forward very delicately and took what appeared to be a modest sip of water from the creek. Stevie smiled. It seemed odd for a horse to make such a ladylike gesture. It made her feel warm all over again about owning the horse. "I can't believe Chelsea changed her mind," she said.

"I can," Carole said. "It turns out she's a nicer person than we thought, that's all. She can admit her mistakes."

"Well, I'm sure glad she did," Stevie said happily.

146

"I guess that makeover we did on the horse turned out to be even more successful than we thought in the end," Stevie mused aloud.

Carole and Lisa nodded. "Even though it didn't keep Chelsea from recognizing her horse, it did show her how much you wanted to keep her," Lisa said.

The mare was now resting contentedly in the shade with the other horses. "So what are you going to do about her name?" she asked Stevie. "Will you start calling her Punk now?"

"No," Stevie said. "I thought about it, and it is funny and sort of appropriate, but it's also kind of ugly. My mare deserves something better. She deserves better than No-Name, too. In fact, from the moment Chelsea told me I could have her, I haven't been able to call her No-Name anymore. It's no better than Punk. I've been thinking about her qualities, the ones I admire, and I'm getting an idea," she said.

"Uh-oh, Stevie's ideas usually get *us* into trouble!" Lisa teased.

"Not this one," Stevie assured her.

"So?" Carole asked.

"Well, it seems to me that this horse may be part Arabian, but she was born here and she's a real Southern belle. I mean, we know she's determined and strong, but she's a beauty and very elegant. Just look at the way she drinks water."

147

As if on cue, the mare stretched her sleek neck to the creek and took another ladylike sip.

Lisa giggled. "She thinks she's at a tea party!"

"Ah think this he-ah hawse is a fahn example of Suthe'n womanhood!" Stevie bellowed in her deepest phony Southern drawl. "She's a true Suthe'n belle and deserves a name to reflect that quality."

Carole and Lisa waited. They knew that Stevie was making up her mind. The answer was about to come.

"Belle," said Stevie.

"It's just right," Carole agreed.

"Has a ring to it," Lisa joked.

Stevie stood up and walked over to her mare. "How are you doing, Belle?" she asked.

The mare regarded her as if she understood this was an important moment. She stood still for a second, almost as if allowing the words to sink in. Then she pawed at the ground with her right hoof and nodded vigorously.

"She likes it!" Stevie declared.

Her horse was named.

"Hi, Belle," Carole said, greeting the mare with her new name.

"Belle!" said Lisa, trying it out herself. "I like it, too."

Stevie smiled proudly. She was pleased with her decision—almost as pleased as she was with owning the horse at all.

"You aren't still mad at Chelsea, are you?" Lisa asked curiously.

"No," Stevie said. "All's well that ends well, and all that. Besides, I'm grateful that she was mature enough to decide to sell Belle back to me. I'm not sure I would have been," she added honestly. Then she frowned. "The one I *am* still mad at is that rat, Veronica. If Chelsea turned out to be a nicer person than we all thought, Veronica turned out to be even more evil than we ever suspected. I checked with Chelsea and sure enough, Veronica told her about the allergy and the bone splint and collected that one-thousand-dollar reward."

"And spent every penny of it, I'll bet, on new riding boots and who knows what else," Carole said. "I don't blame you for being mad at her. I can't believe she was ready to sell you out just so she could keep Garnet nearby."

"It just goes to show that you were right when you said a leopard can't change its spots," Stevie said. "And it confirms what I thought all along—that Veronica diAngelo is a spoiled, rotten, selfish jerk."

"Well, I can't say I like her or anything," Lisa said. "But it was sort of human of her to try to save Garnet like that."

"True," Carole said. "But even though her motives might have been sort of okay for a change, her methods were definitely downright rotten and sneaky."

"I couldn't have said it better myself," Stevie agreed. "Anyway, any hopes we had of Veronica becoming a poorer but better person are gone now." That morning, the girls had learned from Mrs. Reg that Mr. diAngelo's bank had just located the lost papers at the bank and his job was saved—along with the diAngelo fortune. In celebration, Mrs. diAngelo had taken Veronica along to help her pick out a new Mercedes that very day.

"It's too bad," Carole mused. "She was being so friendly there for a while that it was a little weird—but sort of nice at the same time."

"Well, I think it's a relief," Stevie declared. "Now that the regular awful Veronica is back, we won't have to wonder about whether she might have some likable points about her. We can just go back to despising her full time."

Carole and Lisa laughed and agreed.

"Come on," Stevie said, jumping to her feet. "Enough of this sitting around. Let's do some more riding."

She hurried over to untie Belle—her very own horse with her very own name—for the next of their many, many rides together, today and forever.

ABOUT THE AUTHOR

BONNIE BRYANT is the author of more than sixty books for young readers, including novelizations of movie hits such as *Teenage Mutant Ninja Turtles*® *and Honey, I Blew Up the Kid*, written under her married name, B. B. Hiller.

Bonnie Bryant began writing The Saddle Club in 1986. Although she had done some riding before that, she intensified her studies then and found herself learning right along with her characters Stevie, Carole, and Lisa. She claims that they are all much better riders than she is.

Bonnie Bryant was born and raised in New York City. She lives in Greenwich Village with her two sons.

THE SADDLE CLUB™

❏ 15594-6	HORSE CRAZY #1	$3.50/$4.50 Can.	❏ 15938-0	STAR RIDER #19	$3.50/$4.50 Can.
❏ 15611-X	HORSE SHY #2	$3.25/$3.99 Can.	❏ 15907-0	SNOW RIDE #20	$3.50/$4.50 Can.
❏ 15626-8	HORSE SENSE #3	$3.50/$4.50 Can.	❏ 15983-6	RACEHORSE #21	$3.50/$4.50 Can.
❏ 15637-3	HORSE POWER #4	$3.50/$4.50 Can.	❏ 15990-9	FOX HUNT #22	$3.50/$4.50 Can.
❏ 15703-5	TRAIL MATES #5	$3.50/$4.50 Can.	❏ 48025-1	HORSE TROUBLE #23	$3.50/$4.50 Can.
❏ 15728-0	DUDE RANCH #6	$3.50/$4.50 Can.	❏ 48067-7	GHOST RIDER #24	$3.50/$4.50 Can.
❏ 15754-X	HORSE PLAY #7	$3.25/$3.99 Can.	❏ 48072-3	SHOW HORSE #25	$3.50/$4.50 Can.
❏ 15769-8	HORSE SHOW #8	$3.25/$3.99 Can.	❏ 48073-1	BEACH RIDE #26	$3.50/$4.50 Can.
❏ 15780-9	HOOF BEAT #9	$3.50/$4.50 Can.	❏ 48074-X	BRIDLE PATH #27	$3.50/$4.50 Can.
❏ 15790-6	RIDING CAMP #10	$3.50/$4.50 Can.	❏ 48075-8	STABLE MANNERS #28	$3.50/$4.50 Can.
❏ 15805-8	HORSE WISE #11	$3.25/$3.99 Can..	❏ 48076-6	RANCH HANDS #29	$3.50/$4.50 Can.
❏ 15821-X	RODEO RIDER #12	$3.50/$4.50 Can.	❏ 48077-4	AUTUMN TRAIL #30	$3.50/$4.50 Can.
❏ 15832-5	STARLIGHT CHRISTMAS #13	$3.50/$4.50 Can.	❏ 48145-2	HAYRIDE #31	$3.50/$4.50 Can.
❏ 15847-3	SEA HORSE #14	$3.50/$4.50 Can.	❏ 48146-0	CHOCOLATE HORSE #32	$3.50/$4.50 Can.
❏ 15862-7	TEAM PLAY #15	$3.50/$4.50 Can.	❏ 48147-9.	HIGH HORSE #33	$3.50/$4.50 Can.
❏ 15882-1	HORSE GAMES #16	$3.25/$3.99 Can.	❏ 48148-7	HAY FEVER #34	$3.50/$4.50 Can.
❏ 15937-2	HORSENAPPED #17	$3.50/$4.50 Can.	❏ 48149-5	A SUMMER WITHOUT HORSES Super #1	$3.99/$4.99 Can.
❏ 15928-3	PACK TRIP #18	$3.50/$4.50 Can.			

Bantam Doubleday Dell
Books For Young Readers

Bantam Books, Dept. SC35,
2451 South Wolf Road, Des Plaines, IL 60018   DA60

Please send the items I have checked above. I am enclosing $_____ (please add $2.50 to cover postage and handling). Send check or money order, no cash or C.O.D.s please.

Mr/Ms _____

Address _____

City/State _____   Zip _____

Please allow four to six weeks for delivery.
Prices and availability subject to change without notice.   **SC35-4/94**